RENEE'S TRIUMPH

Indrani Sinha

ISBN 978-93-90040-10-0
Copyright © Indrani Sinha, 2020

First published in India 2020 by Inkstate Books
An imprint of Leadstart Publishing Pvt Ltd

Sales Office:
Unit No.25/26, Building No.A/1,
Near Wadala RTO,
Wadala (East), Mumbai – 400037 India
Phone: +91 969933000
Email: info@leadstartcorp.com
www.leadstartcorp.com

Disclaimer: The views expressed in this book are those of the Author and do not pertain to be held by the Publisher.

Editor: Shayoni Mitra
Cover: Ami Parekh
Layouts: Kshitij Dhawale

For all the women who have the strength

to follow their heart

About the Author

Indrani Sinha is a homemaker, who writes in her spare time. She has taught in the Primary section of various schools in different cities. She loves reading, cooking and listening to old Hindi songs. She enjoys going for long nature walks and likes to travel and see new places.

Acknowledgements

This book would not have been possible without the support of my family. Many thanks to my husband Yashvir, for being patient and understanding with me while I took time to keep working at my writing. I am grateful to my son Amitabh and his wife Jamie for always being there for me, whenever I reached out to them. A big thank you to my younger son Atul and his wife Sunaina, who was the first one to read the manuscript and gave me her invaluable suggestions. In addition, Sunaina helped me to download the edited copy of the manuscript, when I did not know how to proceed further and save my work, for which I owe her my gratitude. Authors can be quite bewildered by the working of computers! Finally, I would like to thank all those friends who supported and encouraged me to write and complete this book.

Contents

BOOK ONE

Chapter 1

Lakeview Park

Renee Srivastava was sitting in her room, reading a book, in the railway colony at Alipore in Calcutta in the year 1971. She had given her B.A. exams in Lucknow, where she had been studying, and was with her parents at home waiting for the results to be announced. Lakeview Park was a residential colony meant for senior railway officers, built by the British. Each house was independent, colored a bright brick red with military green border. There was a porch in front which provided shelter in the rainy season, as also from the afternoon sun in the peak summer months. The car was parked in the garage, adjoining each house. There were eighteen houses in all, six in a row. It was a gated colony, with the main entrance from Alipore Road, manned by a security guard.

There was an interesting story behind the name Lakeview. It was said that when the officers from the British Railways came to survey land for a residential colony they saw a small lake in the Alipore area of Calcutta. A junior engineer, wearing a brown *sola topi* and carrying a polished wooden stick, pointed to it and exclaimed loudly, "Oh, what a lake view!" The name stuck. The officers' houses were identical and each was double storied. The porch had eight steps leading up to the main door which opened on to a landing and small sitting area, enclosed by an iron grill. There was a large drawing room to the left of the house with the dining room next to it, with adjacent pantry and kitchen. At the back, along the length of the drawing and dining rooms, was another enclosed verandah, a store room and a bathroom. Behind each house was a small garden with a lawn, which was mostly untended, and which no one ever used. One climbed up a wooden staircase, shining with polish, to reach the upper floor which had three bedrooms with attached bathrooms and an open balcony.

Renee liked the house from the day she saw it. Since she had come home after completing her studies, she was enjoying her holidays spent mostly in the company of her mother or reading books. She had grown into a pretty girl, with a confident bearing. She was five foot four inches tall and kept her hair below shoulder length, which she liked to tie into a plait. Most evenings she would change into her churidar kurta or the single pair of jeans and shirt she owned to go out of the house. She would sit and talk to *Mamoni* for a while in the front verandah while she had her evening tea and then walk over to the Lakeview Club to spend some time there.

The Officer's Club, to the right of the main gate, a single storied building with a huge compound, was meant for use by the railway officers and their families. There were tall hedges planted along the length of the road which gave total privacy to the members. There was a tennis court, where a match would be in progress most evenings. The building itself was modest. It consisted of one large hall with a long verandah running down the front, which had two sets of cane chairs with a centre table each. In front was a lush green lawn with seasonal flowers planted along the edges. Inside, there was a bar where the bearer served soft drinks and potato wafers as no liquor was allowed inside the club. The latest issues of popular magazines were on display on a wooden rack inside the main hall, where one could sit on sofas and read at leisure. There were two card tables: some of the officers were keen bridge players and both tables would most likely be occupied over the weekends. The Club decided to boost its revenue by opening up membership to outsiders; a screening process and interview were put in place before anyone could join. A few corporate executives and young couples had immediately become members to avail the facilities provided.

Rajdeep Varma came every weekend to play tennis. He was fairly tall, of medium build and very agile on the court. He had a pleasant face and equally pleasing manners. When Renee came to the Club, she saw him playing but had not had the opportunity to meet him. About a month into her vacation, Renee was sitting in the verandah, absorbed in reading a magazine. Rajdeep had finished his game of tennis, changed into a fresh T shirt and mopped the sweat off his face and hair.

He walked up to her and introduced himself, "Hello! I'm Rajdeep."

"Oh hello!" she replied. "I'm Renee. I've seen you around here."

He pulled up a chair. "Mind if I sit here? I'm tired. And thirsty. Coca Cola?" he asked.

"Yes, thanks," she nodded.

"Bearer!" he called out loudly, "Two chilled Cokes please."

Renee saw her father, Mr. Brij Mohan Srivastava, walking up the driveway; it was a Saturday evening and he would probably be playing bridge with his friends. She rose as he approached.

"My father," she told Rajdeep.

He was quick on his feet and stretched out his hand, "Hello Sir!"

Offering the distinguished looking gentleman his own seat, he went to fetch another chair, not forgetting to tell the bearer to bring an additional cold drink.

"How are you Rajdeep ? I can see you have introduced yourself to my daughter," remarked her father, sitting on a cane chair.

Renee looked askance, staring from one to the other, "It seems the two of you know each other!" she exclaimed.

Her father smiled, "As a matter of fact, we do."

He had known Rajdeep's father during his College days but had lost touch over the years. It was only when he came to Calcutta this time that they had renewed contact.

"How is your father doing Rajdeep?" he inquired, settling himself on the comfortable chair.

"Working tirelessly at his factory Sir," replied Rajdeep.

Renee's father nodded, "Yes, that's so much like him. Always working hard. And what are you doing, young man?" he asked with interest.

"I work for a tea company, Uncle." Their cold drinks had arrived and they sipped their drinks in silence.

Soon Rajdeep rose to leave; he was hungry and he knew his mother would be waiting for him with a delicious snack. He took his leave and walked briskly to the car park.

About two months later, around the middle of August, the Ladies Welfare Organization of the Railways, held their annual fete on the Club grounds. Food and games stalls had been set up on the spacious lawns. Colorful signs written in red, blue and green on yellow chart paper and pinned on the top of each stall, enticed visitors as they entered the premises: Chatpata Chaat, Hoop the Hoola, Bombay Bhel. Two teenage boys had brought along a portable gramophone from their house and were playing Cliff Richard's "Summer Holiday": the catchy tune of "We're all going on a summer holiday..." filled the air. Entry was restricted to Railway officers and their families and other Club members, and the place was crowded with revellers dressed in colourful clothes, with children dragging their parents to the many games stalls for one more try.

Renee had been observing the preparations being made for the fete on her regular visits to the Club. Sometimes a few aunties would be walking on the grounds pointing out to the supervisors the exact location of the various stalls. The ladies decided on the games and the good cooks among them volunteered to make home made delicacies for the evening. The money collected would be going for the welfare fund of the railway staff and they were all happy to be making a joint effort towards it. The officers' children met in the morning the day before the fete to make the signs on chart papers and Renee joined them. They sat around tables or on the floor, busily writing and colouring, laughing and joking over bowls of potato chips being passed around. There was activity on the lawns too, as the men put up temporary stalls with bamboo poles and multi-coloured canvas cloth.

Renee had been looking forward to the event. Her B.A. results had been announced in July and she was thrilled to have graduated with a first division in English (Honours), although she had just made it past the sixty mark. She felt all grown up and was in a mood to celebrate. She wore a mauve, printed kota sari and the one pair of high heels she had convinced her parents to let her buy from New Market. She put on a matching artificial pearl string she had bought on one of her trips to Halwasiya Market while studying in Lucknow. She brushed her freshly shampood hair till it shone and left it open around her shoulders. She put a small maroon bindi on her forehead and applied the only pink lipstick she owned, which suited her wheatish complexion. She picked up her brown shoulder bag and went to ask *Mamoni* for money.

"I'm going to the Club fete, *Mamoni*," she said, entering her bedroom. "I only have ten rupees...I need some more."

Her mother turned around to look at her and gave a pleased smile. "My daughter has grown up into a beautiful young woman! Only the other day you were running around with your brothers," she remarked as she opened her cupboard to take out the money.

"Here's fifty rupees," she said, handing her the notes. "Now remember to come home before it gets too dark."

"Okay," replied Renee hurriedly, as she picked up her sari folds and concentrated on balancing herself on her heels, and walking carefully out to the upstairs landing area to go down the stairs.

As she walked to the Club, Renee was humming the hit song from the Hindi film *"Aan Milo Sajnaa"* :

Tere karan tere karan

Tere karan mere sajan

Jaag ke phir so gayii

Sapno me kho gaayi..."

Near the Club she saw families excitedly walking to the fete and she followed them inside. She bought coupons worth twenty rupees and went to the Hoop the Gift stall to try her luck. The smiling aunty took coupons worth ten rupees and handed her three hoops and pointed to the array of gifts spread out on the table.

"If you can hoop a gift, it's yours," she explained.

Renee stepped forward and took aim and threw one hoop. It went wide off the mark and fell off the table. A small boy standing next to her sniggered. She ignored him and took another try and missed again. "Oh no, not again!" she exclaimed. "I don't think I can do this."

"No, you surely can," someone spoke from behind her. She turned around to see it was Rajdeep. "Try throwing it sideways and low," he said.

She did as told and the hoop flew from her hand and went to rest over a jam bottle. The boy jumped up and down and clapped his hands joyfully.

The aunty picked up the bottle and handed it to her, "This is yours," she said.

"Thank you," said Renee, taking it and keeping it in her sling bag.

She and Rajdeep went around the stalls and he stopped at Shoot the Target. He gave his coupon and was handed a large toy gun with which he had to hit the red circle at the centre of the target placed at a distance behind the table. He took three tries and missed each time.

He shook his head determinedly, "I'm not leaving like this."

He gave another coupon and aimed the gun, while Renee looked on patiently.

This time he hit the red dot on the second try. "Ha!" he exclaimed loudly, "Got it."

He received his prize of two small chocolates and promptly offered one to Renee.

"Would you like to eat something?" he asked her as he unwrapped his chocolate and bit into it.

"Yes," she nodded, "Let's have some of their delicious home-made chaat." They walked up to the chaat stall and Rajdeep paid with coupons for two plates. They watched as one of the ladies deftly mixed home made crisp papris with boiled potatoes and gram, heaped fresh creamy curd on top, and added green dhaniya and sweet tamarind chutney. She handed them the ready chaat in paper plates with a gracious smile and the two of them moved to one side to savour it.

Renee was sitting with Rajdeep on one of the chairs on the sides of the lawn, when she noticed a young man in his mid-twenties, sitting on a cane chair and watching her with interest. Annoyed, she turned her face away. He was Kunal Chopra, who lived in New Alipore, and had become a member of the Lakeview Club recently. She stared at him angrily. A strong face came into view, with a firm chin and shapely nose. He had a thick mop of hair parted at the side. She could see he was broad shouldered and had crossed his legs as he sat. Angry that someone she did not even know had been staring at her, she swiftly turned her face away. Kunal shrugged his shoulders and stood up to go; she saw he was almost five feet ten inches tall. He went to get himself a coffee from the Espresso stall.

Renee spent the rest of the evening with Rajdeep. She basked in his attention and noticed how courteous he was to her. When it was time to go home, she remembered to thank him for the treats he had given her. As she walked back to her house, she reflected on her carefree childhood, when she could run out, and do whatever she wished to do. As she grew up, she resented the many restrains her parents placed on her freedom because of safety and other issues. She thought longingly of her carefree days in Manduadih railway colony, Varanasi, with her best friends Anita and Sacchu, whom she had left behind, when her father had been transferred to Calcutta and they had all moved to the new city.

Chapter 2
Calcutta

Mr. Srivastava had received his formal transfer orders for Calcutta in March of 1961. He had made a brief trip to check out the accommodation provided for them in the small railway colony, near Sealdah railway station. He had visited a few schools looking for admission for his three children. Back in Manduadih packing began in earnest, and there was the usual chaos in the house. Her two younger brothers Jatin and Sonu, ran around excitedly, trying to lend a helping hand. On the day of their departure, their luggage was loaded on to a truck and the family sat in a station wagon and drove to Mughalsarai station to board their train to Calcutta. Panna ayah gave Renee a tight hug and wiped a tear in her sari pallu as she bid the family farewell. As they left, Renee thought of all the people she was leaving behind: her friends, teachers, and beloved school.

Anita and Sacchu had come to the station to see them off. When they reached Mughalsarai station they walked till the end of the platform, where a saloon was waiting for them, attached to the last bogie of the train. It was the first time Renee and her brothers would be travelling in a saloon, which her father frequently used when he went on official tours. Jatin was the first to scamper up it's steps, followed by Sacchu. "Careful!" her father shouted from behind, even as Renee helped Sonu climb up the steps slowly. Once inside, the boys got busy exploring it's interiors. There was a large compartment with berths to sit on and a dining table with four chairs. Down the corridor were two small bedrooms and bathrooms. The other end of the saloon had a pantry and kitchen. There was a steaming kettle placed on a red hot, coal stove. Renee noticed the netted, wooden "line" box, which contained rice, dal, wheat, sugar and other food items for cooking meals while travelling. While everybody got busy settling the many boxes and trunks, Renee and Anita sat in a corner talking and hoping they would be able to meet sometime in the future. Renee's father asked Anita and Sacchu to alight as it was time for the train to leave. Anita said her goodbyes and alighted but her brother was nowhere to be seen. A frantic search ensued: he was finally discovered hiding behind Jatin, on an upper bunk in one of the bedrooms. The peon hauled him and chased him to the door; Sacchu climbed down the steps just in time, as the engine whistle blew, and their train began to slowly move out of the platform. Renee rushed to the nearest window, tears streaming down her face. Anita waved, while Sacchu ran alongside the train, waving at Renee and her brothers, who were crowding around her. He tripped and fell, rose and waved frantically, as if by doing so he could somehow hold them back.

Mamoni sent for the saloon bearer and asked him to make them some tea and start preparing dinner: aloo gobi curry and pea pulao. The cooks in the saloons turned out mouthwatering fare which was served in fine china with shining cutlery. While her parents had their tea, Renee sat near a window, watching the green countryside and small villages go by. She wondered – What was Calcutta like? She had never been there before but had heard her mother say it was a big and beautiful city. She hoped she would like it, as much as she had enjoyed her stay in Varanasi.

The train reached Howrah station on time and steamed into the huge platform, promptly at eight thirty the next morning. Coolies pushed their way inside the coaches, to bring out the luggage of the arriving passengers. As she alighted Renee saw the platform was teeming with people: entire families were waiting to catch the next train, sitting patiently near their baggage, eating jhal muri and roasted peanuts. There was a carriageway for vehicular transport between platform numbers eight and nine. This was a unique facility which allowed passengers to be dropped or picked up from near train compartments. There were many cars parked on either side of the road waiting to receive passengers, and Renee and her family sat in a station wagon into which their luggage had already been loaded.

The driver drove their vehicle to the front main road of the station, turned left and then took a right turn towards Howrah bridge. Renee had seen it once in a Hindi movie and asked *Mamoni* about it. "It's grand," her mother had replied, "The British built it and it connects Howrah to Calcutta city."

"Look *Didi!*" Jatin shouted, tugging at her sleeve, "A man pulling a rickshaw."

Renee was shocked to see three such hand pulled rickshaws with the passengers sitting comfortably on the seats, while lean looking men ran holding on to wooden bars extending on either side.

"This is so cruel *Mamoni!*"she cried, "Why are they running like this?"

Her mother replied calmly, "They are called hand pulled rickshaws, Renee. These men earn a living doing this and support their families."

Howrah bridge had broad pavements on either side of the road, with sturdy iron railings which separated it from the busy main road. The footpath was teeming with people, many of whom were walking briskly, while some others were speeding past on bicycles. There were hawkers sitting with open baskets selling flowers, peanuts, bags and purses and a few people were stopping to look at them and buy them.

They crossed the bridge and drove into a broad avenue called Strand Road which had tall, majestic buildings on both sides. Calcutta was called the City of Palaces. It had been the capital, during the days of the British Raj, when the Governor General resided here. Most of the British mercantile firms had their headquarters in Calcutta during those early days. The façade of the buildings on Strand Road had exquisite marble carvings, massive stone pillars and quaint balconies. The footpath was crowded with men hurrying to work, dressed in dhoti kurta or shirt and trousers, many of them carrying bags and umbrellas tucked under their arm.

They reached the railway guest house and were shown to their rooms. The children were all tired after the train journey and quickly set about opening their toothbrushes and toothpastes while *Mamoni* ordered breakfast for them. Next morning Renee and her father left in a taxi, to seek admission for her in a girls school in Acharya Jagdish Chandra Bose Road. When they alighted they found the large, green iron gate firmly shut. A durwan popped out from a green colored, wooden window of the guard room next to the gate, and inquired the purpose of their visit. Renee's father told him they had an appointment with the Principal. He requested them to wait outside, while he quickly ran inside to check; he returned a few minutes later and unlocked the massive gate to let them inside.

Renee felt apprehensive as they walked to the large administrative building, on the right side of the compound. They were greeted by a peon, dressed in khaki pant and shirt, who ushered them into the Principal's office. It was a big room with many windows overlooking the garden, and a cupboard full of books. Renee noticed the large glass display cabinet which had various trophies and cups the students had won in sports and other inter-school competitions. The Principal was busy correcting exercise books piled to one side of the large table. When they came in, she looked up, closed the copy she had been checking, put her red pen on the table and asked the father and daughter to take their seats. She was a well built lady with her hair cut in a short bob and was wearing a printed dress.

"Tell me," she said, "How can I help you?"

Her father introduced himself and told her that he had recently come to Calcutta on a transfer and was seeking admission for his daughter in her prestigious school. Renee's grades were good and after a perfunctory glance at the report card and transfer certificate the Principal pressed the bell for her secretary. A young woman, smartly dressed in a navy blue pencil skirt and cream coloured blouse, immediately opened the door and came inside the room. The Principal instructed her to grant admission to Renee in class six. She rose, indicating the meeting was over. When she spoke, her voice was gentle and her smile warm. "Renee," she said, "I hope you are going to enjoy studying in our school."

She did too: yet it was all so different from her previous school in Varanasi. On her first day in school her father dropped her outside the gate, crowded by students and their guardians. Renee walked inside nervously, clutching her school bag and stared at the happy and eager girls, wearing their uniform of yellow blouse, dark green skirt and green tie, laughing and talking excitedly with each other. Renee felt lost and wished she was back in Varanasi with her friends in her old school. Suddenly, someone tapped her on her left shoulder. Surprised, she spun around to see a bright eyed girl, slightly taller than her, with a wide smile on her face.

"New here?" she inquired.

"Yes," replied Renee, nodding her head.

"Hi!" the girl said brightly, "I'm Elizabeth. They call me Lizzie. I study in class six. And you?"

"I'm Renee. I study in class six too," she said, filled with trepidation by the noise around her.

"Come with me!" Lizzie caught hold of her hand and lead her quickly along the compound, dodging groups of chattering girls, and up a crowded staircase, along a long corridor till they reached their classroom. It was a large room with individual desks and chairs laid out in neat rows and windows along the length of the wall. There was loud laughter and animated talk as the girls came in one by one and greeted each other.

A girl was standing near the blackboard, writing something on it with white chalk and then, as quickly, erasing it.

Lizzie raised her hand commandingly and there was immediate silence; she was quite the class leader.

"We have a new girl in our class...I want all of you to meet Renee Srivastava!" she announced grandly, with a flourish of her hands.

The girls chorused in one voice, "Hi Renee! Welcome to our class."

They were full of eager questions, "Where have you come from? Where do you live? Can you speak Bengali?"

Before Renee could answer them, the bell rang, sharp and clear. The noise stopped immediately and the girls ran to their respective seats.

Mrs. Biswas, their Hindi teacher, wearing a brown handloom sari, hair piled high in a bun, appeared at the door. She was holding a textbook and some exercise books in her hands. She greeted them, took their attendance, and began the day's lesson. She asked them to open page seven, went to the blackboard, and wrote in Hindi:

Moti ek kutta hai

Moti ke do kaan hain

Renee yawned; she had studied Hindi of a much higher standard in Varanasi. This is going to be so easy, she thought. She would find out soon, though, that all the other subjects were much tougher and she would need to work hard to catch up to the level.

Rudra, her father's office peon, appeared near the school gate at three in the afternoon, when school gave over for the day. He was a burly man, wore cotton shirt and trousers, and on his feet he had a pair of rough looking sandals. He had an inscrutable look on his face which never betrayed any emotion. As Renee emerged from the school gate, he took her bag and silently beckoned her to follow him. He led her away from the medley of students and their parents and guardians who had come to collect them. They quickly walked past street hawkers selling chaat, puchka, and churan towards what seemed like a rail track on one side of the wide road. Renee watched in amazement as a train consisting of two coaches, came towards them with it's bell clanging loudly. A tram! As it came to a halt at it's scheduled stop to pick up passengers, Rudra motioned to her to climb in. She took a seat near a window in the third row; he sat two rows behind her and bought tickets for the two of them. Renee was soon to learn that this was a not a train but a tram and was going to be the mode of transport by which she returned home from her school every afternoon.

Although Rudra escorted her home every day, she never needed to speak to him even once. Silence has its own language. She always felt safe with him and after alighting from the tram near Sealdah railway station, he made it a point to walk with her through the railway colony, right up to their flat. He left for office only when the door was opened by someone from inside the house, and she had gone in. He never betrayed her trust, unlike *Somenda*, whom she had begun to trust and who broke her faith in him.

CHAPTER 3
LOSS OF INNOCENCE

The small Railway colony in Sealdah consisted of four cream colored apartment buildings, each four stories high. Every floor had two adjacent flats with a staircase running down the middle. Renee hated the new place from the day they moved in; she missed her friends Anita and Sacchu, the wide open spaces, the green lawns and the vegetable garden of their Manduadih bungalow. They lived on the first floor of one of the buildings. Their new home was a two bedroom flat with a combined drawing cum dining room and a long, open balcony in front, where she liked to stand and breathe in the fresh air. Her brothers studied in a different school and went by bus, which picked them up every morning and dropped them back in the afternoon.

Jatin was frequently up to some mischief in the house. One afternoon, the flat was unusually quiet: *Mamoni* was taking her nap, and Renee and Sonu were in their bedroom playing ludo. Suddenly, she felt thirsty and went to drink a glass of water. She let out a scream as soon as she walked into the kitchen _ Jatin was standing in front of the sink, holding one hand under running tap water, which was turning into a bright pink. Blood. She ran to her mother's room yelling,

"*Mamoni! Mamoni!* Come quickly....Jatin has cut his hand and it's bleeding badly. Hurry!" Her mother almost jumped out of bed and the two of them ran to the kitchen. Jatin was still standing there, his hand under the running tap, hoping the bleeding would somehow stop.

"What are you doing?" his mother shouted.

"I cut my hand," he said, "trying to cut out the wheels and axle from that car." A broken plastic car and sharp blade lay on the kitchen counter.

"Are you crazy?" asked his sister, petrified at the sight of so much blood.

Her mother rushed to the railway phone to call up her husband. She tied a piece of cloth tightly around his finger. Father was home in five minutes and, furious though he was, wasted no time in bundling him downstairs into his car and taking him to the emergency room of the railway hospital nearby. Jatin returned half an hour later, looking somewhat pale, but nevertheless feeling heroic, with a large bandage on his finger. Renee and Sonu fussed over him, his mother made him his favourite drink of hot chocolate and father, went back to office.

Gradually Renee started liking her new school. She learnt a lot, and her school assignments kept her occupied at home in the evenings. Recess time in school was always fun and riotous. The girls never seemed to walk: they jumped, skipped or ran. They bumped against each other and continued on their way: no one seemed to mind, as they greeted each other cheerfully. Renee, polite and well-mannered to a fault, secretly admired their confidence and wished she could be more boisterous like them.

Back in Sealdah Railway Colony, children of all ages came outdoors on most evenings and played various games: seven tiles and gully cricket being favourites. The older girls would sit on one of two cement benches, exchanging news. That's where Renee met Chhotdi, who was studying in a College in the city. She came from a conservative Bengali family, and her father was a section officer in the Sealdah divisional office. They should never have been friends in the first place, considering that Renee was still a school girl, not yet in her teens, while Chhotdi was a young woman, much older than her.

One evening, during their usual rendezvous within the Colony, *Chotdi* had said to her, "You're growing up pretty, Renee... you remind me of the Hindi film actress Nutan." Renee had no idea what she was talking about, although she had seen the famous actress in a movie she had watched with her parents. She had stared at her for some time, not knowing what to say. She racked her brains for a befitting rejoinder; a thought struck her, and she rose from the bench where they had been sitting, and remarked, "And you remind me of Audrey Hepburn," before running off to play with her friends.

Renee was so free spirited and independent minded that her mother found it difficult to handle her as she grew into a teenager. She warned her daughter to stop playing with the boys, and to come home early, but to no avail. Renee herself saw that most of the girls returned home as soon as dusk fell. Instead of returning to the safe confines of her home, she would linger on playing, and only go home when the last few children went back. Later on in her life, she wished that her parents had been been stricter with her and had set time limits. It was not long before she learnt her lesson that young girls should not wander around unescorted late in the evenings; some man could take advantage of them.

She celebrated her twelfth birthday that May. Days flew by and school activities kept Renee and her brothers busy. In October, the festival of Durga Puja was being celebrated in Calcutta with great enthusiasm and joy. The children residing in the colony began preparing for a variety entertainment program to be performed in front of their parents. Donations were collected from all the residents and a proper stage with arrangements for lighting and mike were set up. Renee and two other girls were learning a poem "Jhansi ki Rani" to be recited, with actions, on that day. Chairs had been placed in the Puja pandal for the audience to sit. On the evening of the program, most of the parents turned up to watch but Renee's father and mother did not come. Her father was working late at the office and *Mamoni* refused to come alone. The show started, and half an hour later, it was their turn to go on stage. The three of them wearing colorful shararas, kurtis and dupattas, bright red lipstick on their innocent lips, trooped out and greeted the audience with folded hands.

They began their recitation well enough:

"Bundeley Harbolon keh munh hamney suni kahani thi,

Khoob ladi mardani woh to Jhansi wali Rani thi…………."

Renee saw the huge crowd of spectators sitting in front of her, and all of a sudden, fear gripped her heart and she could not utter a single word. She stood on the stage staring at them, speechless and paralysed by fear; it seemed as though her voice had frozen. She tried her best to speak but it seemed her lips would not move. She stood in front of all the people, feeling ashamed.

One of the girls by her side, who had continued with her recitation, paused for a moment and hissed, "Why have you stopped?"

Renee could take it no more and ran tearfully backstage, bumping into her friend Chhotdi, who had been watching their performance from behind the wings. Her elder brother, Somen, was with her, helping out with the stage lighting.

"Renee!" he asked, his voice full of concern, "What happened to you? You were so good at practice this morning."

"Sorry *Somenda!*" she replied in a trembling voice, "I could not remember my lines." She looked crestfallen, as she stood there, feeling the pain of being a failure, while her friends continued performing on stage, in front of an appreciative audience.

"It's all right," Chhotdi said, putting her arms around her and leading her out. Renee's brothers Jatin and Sonu had been in the audience watching their sister's humiliation but neither of them mentioned it to their parents over dinner that night. Soon Renee forgot all about the embarrassing incident and plunged whole heartedly into her school work.

After their support to her that evening, she began to trust Chhotdi and her brother. In the evenings she would often be sitting on one of the cement benches with the other girls when *Somenda* would return from office on his scooter. He must have been twenty one or twenty two years old and had only recently begun working at his first job, after completing his graduation. He was well built, fairly tall and had a pleasant face.

"*Somenda! Somenda!*" she would go running up to greet

him, as soon as he got down and wheeled his scooter to the parking lot near his apartment building.

"And how are you Renee?" he would ask, stopping midway to talk to her.

"Oh, I had a very busy day in school..." she would answer quickly, and promptly go running back to join her friends.

Somen was a good ten years older than her, and in the prime of his youth. At twelve, Renee who was still a child, had absolutely no idea that she was asking for trouble, by constantly going to him looking for friendship and approval. Early in January the following year, she was walking back home after seeing off a friend to her apartment building close to the main gate. It was already dusk on a cold winter evening and she was in a hurry to get home. Not many people were around as Somen returned from work and parked his scooter.

He spotted Renee alone on the road and called out to her.

"Come here Renee!" he called, waving his hand at her, "I want to show you something."

"Not today *Somenda*," she replied, walking up to him. "It's getting late and I'm cold and hungry," she said, shivering and wrapping her shawl tightly around her.

"Come, come," he insisted, "It'll only take a minute." Not knowing how to refuse, she followed him obediently. He walked up to the back boundary wall and bent forward to show her a lighted diya through a latticed window. As Renee bent to see what he was showing, she felt a warm, soft hand cup her tender right breast. He had slipped his hand under her shawl and was touching her breast. Shocked and frightened, she pushed him back so hard he almost tripped and fell, and ran all the way home, ringing the doorbell insistently till their bungalow peon opened the door. Her parents were in the drawing room: her father was reading the newspaper and *Mamoni* was knitting a sweater. She did not go to them, nor did she tell them about her traumatic experience. She went straight to her bedroom, where the sight of her two younger brothers playing a card game calmed her. She could feel her heart thumping and she was shaking in fear.

Jatin noticed something was wrong and came and stood by her side. "*Didi?*" he asked with concern. He could see his sister was very upset.

" You go and play with Sonu, I'll be fine," she whispered, sitting on the bed. She lay down and curled up, closing her eyes and trying to shut out the incident and Somen's face. She was frightened at what he had tried to do with her and it took some time before she had composed herself enough to pick up and start reading her Enid Blyton book. It was the loss of innocence for Renee, and she grew up overnight. She understood she could never trust a man, and she made up her mind to keep a distance from them in the future.

Renee did not go near *Somenda* and stopped talking to Chhotdi, when she went to the play area downstairs next evening. She was immensely relieved when her father announced, a few days later, that he had been transferred to far away Liluah Railway Colony. They were being allotted a large upper floor flat in a double storeyed bungalow; in addition, there was a huge lawn in front of their new house. There followed the usual flurry of packing and fetching transfer certificates for the children, to be used for admission in their new schools. Renee was happy to leave Sealdah Railway Colony. She did not look back even once as their black Landmaster car drove off, and she never saw or heard of Somen again.

CHAPTER 4

LILUAH

Liluah is a small town five kilometers North of Howrah. It's history dates back to the British era when the Liluah Carriage and Wagon Workshop was set up by the British Railways. A township was planned and built for the British officers, called the Liluah Railway Colony, where they lived with their families. The roads were given the names of the British engineers who worked in the workshops and almost the entire colony was surrounded by a boundary wall. Most of the officers lived on Gardiner Road, which had large double storied houses with huge lawns; at the back were the garage and the servants quarters. There was an Officer's Club on the same road, with tennis and badminton courts and other basic facilities. There were parallel roads on either side of Gardiner Road which had apartment buildings where the section officers and support staff stayed.

Their new apartment on the upper floor of a bungalow seemed like a tree house to Renee at first. She had a small room to herself with long, shuttered windows, colored a soothing dark green, which she opened in the evenings during the hot summer months, to let in the cool breeze. The branches of a mango tree growing next to it touched the windows;

it was so close one could break a few leaves by stretching out the hand. The apartment on the ground floor had been allotted to another officer and he lived there with his family. Their elder son studied in Oak Grove, a boarding school in Jharipani near Mussourie, meant only for children of railway officers. The younger one Deepak, was Jatin's age and they studied in the same boys school close by and it wasn't long before the two of them became good friends. There was a huge, unkempt lawn in front of their house, with a long driveway from the gate, lined by trees and bushes, leading up to the house.

Their's was the first bungalow on Gardiner Road; beyond its boundary wall, across the public road, was a large pond. All the four children were playing in the garden one lazy, Saturday afternoon. Renee watched as Jatin and Deepak whispered to each other, pointing to the pond. They seemed to have come to a decision: in a moment they had run out of the gate and were crossing the main road, with Sonu in hot pursuit. Alarmed, Renee shouted, "Jatin, where are you going?" On an impulse, she decided to follow them. When she caught with up them, the three were standing under a neem tree and watching men and women bathing and washing clothes in the pond. There was a group of young boys frolicking and splashing handfuls of water at each other. All of a sudden, Jatin ran into the water and Sonu joined him. They began wading into the shallow side, with the water reaching their calf level.

Renee cried, "Jatin, what are you doing? Come out, both of you! You don't know how to swim!"

She watched in horror as Sonu began to gradually sink, and thrashed his arms in the water.

Jatin desperately tugged at Sonu's shirt sleeve and yelled, "Help...my brother is drowning!"

Renee ran up and down the bank screaming, "Jaldi karo... someone help!"

Two men swimming close by reached him swiftly, and dragged him out. Sonu was in a state of shock and stood there shivering, holding his hands close to his chest, as the water dripped off his clothes. Jatin had stepped out of the water earlier and he, too, was shaking with cold and fear. Renee remembered to thank the two men who had saved her brother, and the frightened children ran all the way home. To say the least, *Mamoni* was distressed at their misadventure and sent them off for baths and a change of dry clothes. They felt better after they had bathed and eaten toast, butter and jam and had a glass of milk. Their father was furious when he returned from office that evening, and heard about it, and forbade them from stepping on to the public road again.

Renee loved her new school, St Agnes' Convent School in Howrah, from day one. It was located about five miles from her house, situated in a narrow lane off the Grand Trunk Road. The G.T. road carried heavy traffic through the day with trucks ferrying goods from all over the country, buses carrying workers to various manufacturing units in Liluah, cars, rickshaws and hand carts. Their school bus picked up the students staying in Gardiner Road, Pearce Road and another road in the huge Lilluah Railway Colony at eight in the morning and dropped them off in the afternoon.

Their school gate was kept half closed at any given time, so no vehicles could go inside without the Principal's permission. The school building was a grey coloured, three storied structure with crimson borders. Inside the large hall in front, which one entered through a porch, was a stage made of polished mahogany wood, with thick maroon velvet curains, where assembly was conducted every morning. A grand piano stood in a slanting position near the entrance door, on which their music teacher played a Western music tune every morning after assembly, for the girls to march into their classrooms. They went down a long corridor, which had the Principal's office to the left and the staffroom directly opposite, and kept walking in line and entered their respective classrooms, six and seven being on the ground floor. They climbed up a spiral, iron staircase to reach classes eight and above, located on the second floor. In addition, the upper floor had the school chapel, the library, needle work room and a fully equipped science laboratory.

The girls wore a half sleeved, green dress with cape collars; a green cotton belt worn over their dress and button-on team tie completed their uniform. There were fifteen of them in her class, and although they came from diverse cultural backgrounds, they bonded well and became good friends. It was eventually Sara, who became her best friend, and who helped her regain some of her confidence again. Sara Tandon was very attractive, slim, good in the humanities subjects and excelled in quite a few extra-curricular activities. Renee was sharp, bright and did extremely well in the science subjects, and participated in dramatics and debates. Sara enjoyed playing basketball; Renee disliked it.

When they were studying in class eight, Renee was running across the cemented basketball court during recess when Sara, who had been watching her from a distance, yelled, "Renee you're putting on weight!"

Renee did an about turn, and came charging back at her friend, "How dare you Sara! Call me fat, will you?"

Sara chuckled, "See yourself in the mirror…..watch your weight, Renee."

In the privacy of her bedroom that evening, Renee stood in front of the mirror and examined herself; her friend had been right. She was indeed putting on weight. She wanted to remain slim and active, and began to watch her diet from that day, having less of sweets and other fattening food. It became a lifetime habit for her.

When they were studying in class nine, they fought over the length of their noses, one afternoon. They were both eating lunch in the elongated tin shed, in front of the basketball court. "Your nose is too long," Renee commented thoughtfully, examining her friend's profile, as she bit into her delicious vegetable paratha roll.

"Nonsense!" replied Sara furiously, "Look at yours."

"Mine is just right," replied Renee primly, taking another bite of the paratha. "Besides, it suits me."

Sara was eating her fried rice. She paused. "What makes you think mine doesn't suit me? It's nice and acquiline. My father says I have a nice nose. To me that's all that matters."

"O.K." replied Renee, "I like mine better."

The two girls paused, stared at each other, and burst out laughing. They were best friends indeed, there was no doubt about that.

Mr.Srivastava got a promotion and they shifted to a double

storied house in Gardiner Road with a lawn, and servants quarters at the back. The children enjoyed playing in the lawn, which had barbed wire and a green hedge along the boundary. There were many trees which provided shade in the summer season. The house itself was big with a grand wooden staircase, with gleaming bannisters, leading to the upper floors, which had two bedrooms, with attached dressing rooms and bathrooms. The drawing and dining rooms were on the ground floor, as also a guest room and bathroom, in addition to the pantry and kitchen. During their school holidays, Jatin asked his sister one morning to help him haul the portable gramophone to the front lawn; the duo went to the guest room where it was kept on a side table and carried it to the lawn, where they placed it gently on the soft grass. Jatin went inside and came running back with a few old records from their father's collection. Brimming with excitement, he wound the gramophone and played a record: the music was slow and the singing monotonous and it was quickly discarded. Helped by his sister, he kept trying till they hit upon a catchy tune. Their friends heard the loud music and came to join them. As they surrounded him, Jatin importantly placed a 78 rpm record on the turnstile and put the needle carefully on it. Immediately the melodious voices of Ashok Kumar and Devika Rani filled the air:

"Main ban ki chidiya ban ke ban ke ban ban boloon re

Main ban ka panchi ban ke sang sang doloon re………………."

The song was from the Hindi film Achyut Kanya made in 1936.

All of a sudden, Jatin climbed up a mango tree and began shaking a branch vigorously each time the words "doloon re...." was sung. All their friends burst into peals of laughter. The friends took turns winding the gramophone and playing the records. *Mamoni* appeared at the verandah and shouted at them to stop the din and come back inside. No one listened to her. Renee quickly went inside and brought out a big, round box of J.B. Mangharam biscuits. She opened the lid, took out one orange cream biscuit, licked the cream and bit into the crunchy edge. Once outside, she offered everyone the biscuits which they gatefully accepted and devoured hungrily. People passing by, looked on at the kids and smiled. A gentle wind blew; the day was pleasant and all was well with the world.

One of the highlights of Renee's holidays was the Sunday lunch at Kwality restaurant in Park Street. The children would eagerly pile into the back seat of their Landmaster car, even as *Mamoni* sat in the passenger seat, and their father would drive through the busy Grand Trunk Road to Calcutta. They crossed Howrah bridge, then drove on to Strand Road and finally emerged on to the immensely smooth and broad expanse of Red Road. Renee had been fascinated to learn that fighter planes had taken off and landed on it during World War two; it was still used every year for the grand parade on 26th January. On the left they could see the vast Maidan, the lungs of the city, and people strolling and enjoying the outdoors.

Their car took a left turn and they entered Park Street: the ultimate destination for glamour and glitz in Calcutta. It had beautiful buildings on either side of the wide road, high-end stores and the best restaurants in the city. There was a broad sidewalk with metal railings on either side of the road, meant for pedestrian use. Sitting in her Landmaster car Renee admired the handsome men in lounge suits, escorting beautiful ladies wearing chiffon saris and pearl strings, and walking gracefully in their high heels. Some of the women wore dresses and skirts and all carried fancy handbags. How Renee wished her mother was fashionable like these women! She decided that when she grew up she was going to wear gorgeous saris, carry an expensive leather purse and look so glamorous in her heels that everyone would stop to admire her.

Her father had parked their car and Jatin gave her a nudge, saying rudely, "Hurry! What are you waiting for? Open the door."

"So don't push me," she retorted angrily, opening the door and stepping out.

They went inside Kwality restaurant, which had a simple décor, with tables and chairs laid out on both sides of an elongated room. Once they were seated the steward came to take their order. Renee's father ordered his favourite dishes: tandoori chicken, chole and naan. The food arrived soon and Renee broke off pieces of the soft naan and ate it with the delicious chicken and chole. Dessert was ice cream and Renee waited eagerly for the waiter to ask her, and she ordered the same one each time: strawberry. Once the bill was paid, they would troop outside and her parents would order paan from the famous corner shop: "meetha " for father and "zarda" for *Mamoni*. They would be bundled into the car for the long drive home; a warm, secure feeling enveloped Renee, as she leant back contentedly on her seat, and looked out at Park Street as their car wound its way home through the traffic.

Once the summer holidays were over, Renee fell into the regular rhythm of academics. When she was studying in class ten, Sara and she had been chosen Vice Captain of Green and Blue teams respectively. Renee took her new responsibility seriously, lining up the girls for Assembly each morning, checking their uniform or straightening a tie. Studies were absorbing and she embarked on each new lesson as an adventure. She had taken up the science stream but dropped biology in class ten because she could not go through the dissection of cockroaches and frogs. The first time she did one, she rushed to the wash basin, and puked. She took up higher Maths and discovered her fear of trigonometry; it was only her teacher's patience which helped her cope with it. Physics and Chemistry fascinated her and she began enjoying laboratory work. Strange that after this, Renee should decide to study English Honours for her graduation course. Perhaps she became aware of the fact that a scientist was not what she was meant to be.

Renee would walk up to the Officer's Club most evenings, hoping to meet a friend or to read her favourite magazines and have Coca Cola. She had learnt a life lesson at a tender age in Sealdah railway colony, and she made sure never to be alone with any strange man and to return home as soon as dusk fell. A young man introduced himself to her one evening; he said he lived outside the colony and his name was Dilip. Having completed his graduation, he was searching for a job, and had come here to meet his college friend who happened to be a Railway officer's son. He persisted in striking up a conversation and Renee happened to mention that she liked The Beatles and Cliff Richard.

Next evening, when she reached the Club, Dilip was already there, waiting for her. He greeted her warmly and handed her a small packet. "What's this?" she asked, taken completely by surprise.

"It's a gift for you," he said, smiling. "Go ahead. Open it."

"I can't take this," she protested, handing him back the thin square envelope. "I hardly know you."

"It isn't anything expensive. I want you to listen to the songs," he assured her, "two records.....of your favourite singers."

She jumped with joy. "The Beatles! Cliff Richard!" She began tearing the wrapping paper excitedly and pulled out two 45rpm records. She held on to them tightly: she was not going to let them go.

"Thank you so much," she said, "This is so nice of you."

"I'm glad you like these, Renee. I hope you enjoy listening to them too."

She skipped all the way home, packet clutched tightly in her hands.

Mamoni was upstairs and father had not yet returned from office. Her brothers were eating toast and jam in the dining room. She went straight to the radiogram in the drawing room and began playing "Summer Holiday"; just then her father arrived from the office and parked his car in the porch.

Mr. Brij Mohan Srivatava alighted from his car and Umer Singh promptly appeared to take his briefcase and lunch box, which he carried inside the house. Renee's father stood for a while on the entrance steps, puzzled by the sound of music blaring from inside the house. As he strode in, he was aghast to see his teenage daughter dancing with gay abandon in the drawing room.

"Renee!" he shouted, "Stop this at once."

Renee had not heard her father's car arriving, and was shocked to see him suddenly standing there, and glaring at her. Afraid, she stood still.

"Where did you get these records?"

"A boy gave them to me," she answered timidly.

"Which boy?" he asked angrily.

"Dilip," she whispered, her voice barely audible.

"Who is he?" her interrogation continued.

"He lives outside the colony... I met him at the Club yesterday. I told him I liked The Beatles and Cliff Richard..."

"So he presented these records to you," her father interrupted her, furious that she had accepted the gift from a stranger. "Return them at once!"

Renee looked up at him. "Why," she asked, "What wrong did I do?"

"Don't argue with me. You're too young to understand what is wrong about this, Renee," he said. "Return these records to him tomorrow evening."

Renee did as she was told, but failed to understand what had made her father so angry. She still had a lot of growing up to do, and it would be many years she before she understood the devious workings of the world.

CHAPTER 5

RENEE AND SARA

Renee was sixteen years old in 1968 and in her final year in school. When they were studying in class ten, Sara Tandon and Renee Srivastava had been chosen as Vice Captains of the Green team and Blue team. The next year when they were promoted to their Senior Cambridge class they became Captains of their respective teams. Two other girls from their class were chosen to lead the red and yellow teams. Renee felt very important standing at the head of her team at Assembly each morning, and she took her new responsibility seriously, making sure the students followed all school rules.

Classes were on in full swing, when Sister Sophie, their Principal and also English teacher, gave them home-work to do: to write the precis of a passage in Wren and Martin, their grammar textbook. Many of the girl forgot about it, and copied hurriedly from Cecilia in class next morning. The bell rang, they ran back to their desks, took out their exercise books and awaited Sister Sophie's arrival, each of the girls looking a picture of innocence. When Sister Sophie walked into class a few minutes later, the girls stood up and greeted her, "Good Morning Sister!"

"Good morning girls," replied Sister Sophie taking her seat, and arranging her books on the table in front of her. She took out her red pen and said, "Sit down and bring me your exercise books one by one for checking."

The first one to go with her exercise book open on the precis page was Rita. She stood obediently, her hands behind her back, as Sister carefully read her work, gave it a right tick, signed and dated it. As the girls walked up to her desk with their work and Sister Sophie continued checking their exercise books, her face went pale. She opened the copies and placed the precis next to each other, checking the paragraphs again. The were all exactly the same, word for word. Furious, she stood up. "Cheats!" she cried, "You have copied from each other. Did you not?"

Two girls immediately stood up protesting loudly, "No Sister, we did it at home last evening."

"I believe you," Sister reassured them. "Sit down, you two." She looked at the other girls, who were all looking down, staring at their desks, observing the intricacies of the wood. "Stand up, rest of the class," she spoke calmly, "Tell me truthfully, did you also write your precis last evening at home?"

There was stunned silence, as the girls rose and stood quietly. No one spoke.

"Speak up," Sister continued, "You have a voice. I need an answer, Yes or No."

"No Sister," they cried in unison, looking at her, with guilt showing on their faces.

"I want to know from whom you have all copied this precis."

"From me Sister," Cecilia said tearfully, owning up.

Sister Sophie rose from her chair, gathered her pen and text books, and began walking towards the door, where she paused and said, "You are the Senior Cambridge class. I am ashamed of you." Before leaving the classroom, she announced, "Don't bother to come to school from tomorrow."

The girls could only stare at her in shock and horror.

"We can't go home and tell this to our parents," one of the girls said, bursting into tears, "This can't be true....we have our Senior Cambridge exams in November."

"Stop crying," said Renee. "It won't solve our problem. We have to say sorry to Sister. She's very upset with us."

"We have to apologize immediately," agreed Sara, "Let's go."

They walked in line to the Principal's office and asked the Secretary, Mrs. Ryan, a petite woman wearing a yellow blouse and brown pleated skirt, to let them meet Sister Sophie. Sister Sophie had left word not to let them in. Mrs. Ryan, trying hard not to smile at seeing their consternation, politely and firmly told the girls Sister was very busy and could not possibly see them, so could they please return to class.

They went back upstairs silently and sat in their seats quietly. The bell rang for the next period and they took out their Math book and waited anxiously for their teacher, Miss Jennifer, to appear. No one came. Rita went downstairs to the staff room to check and was told she was not free. It was already two thirty in the afternoon and the last period of the day; the girls knew they could not go home and give such disastrous news to their mothers. At three, the peon rang the dispersal bell, clanging it for a few extra seconds. A murmur of excitement arose, as students in various classes got busy stuffing their books into their bags to go home.

Their was a rush of activity around the school gate as parents and gaurdians picked up the girls, some of whom crowded around the chaatwallah for some aloo chaat, others wanted orange ice lolly. Amidst all this confusion, the students of the Senior Cambridge class stood to one side, looking forlorn; they saw the two school buses leave. They decided to walk to the bank of the river Hoogly close by, and figure out their next course of action. It was a short walk, on the left side of their school building and soon they could see the majestic river flowing calmly. As they stood on the mounds of grass, they could see an entire city in front of them, the city of Calcutta, which lay across the river Hoogly. It was quiet and peaceful on the river bank, with a few men lying on the cool grass and resting. They threw their bags on the ground and sat on the green grass stretching out their legs, and felt the cool breeze on their faces. One could see the grand Howrah bridge, connecting the two cities of Howrah and Calcutta, and boats bobbing in the distant waters.

 The girls faced the unpleasant truth that Sister Sophie was still angry with them and refusing to meet them as well.

"I know what we have to do!" cried Rita excitedly, "Let's go and say sorry to Mother Superior. She'll meet us."

"Yes! Yes!" there was an immediate chorus. Hurriedly, they picked up their bags and almost ran all the way back to school. The amused durwan let them in, even though it was well past school hours. The school was deserted, except for the gardener tending to the potted plants and the cleaners sweeping the front yard. Jessie, the old woman who stayed within the premises, cackled to see the senior girls in trouble. The girls went up the spiral staircase and rushed to meet Mother Superior who was still in her office, completing some important work. Mother Superior, who was a diminutive figure, exuding grace and courage, came out of her room immediately.

"Yes?" she inquired, in a steady and firm voice.

"Good afternoon Mother," Sara greeted her. "You must have heard Sister Sophie is very angry with us. She has told us not to come to school from tomorrow."

"….We have our Senior Cambridge exams this year, Mother," Cecelia interrupted her friend, "We can't go back home like this."

"First things first," asked Mother Superior calmly, "What did you do to deserve such a punishment?"

"We did something wrong, Mother," said Sara, speaking for all of them. "We cheated."

"We've come to say sorry," said Renee. "We won't do such a thing again."

"Please let us meet Sister Sophie once!" pleaded Rita.

"Sister is very angry," Mother Superior admonished them sternly.

"Sorry Mother!" the girls cried in unison, looking contrite.

"All right," replied Mother Superior. "Never do this again. You may come to school from tomorrow."

Relieved, the girls smiled and broke into excited chatter: it had been an eventful day, and one they would remember for the rest of their lives. For now, they were worried about returning home. A few of the girls who lived close by, said their goodbyes and began walking home, while others decided to take hand rickshaws. Renee and Sara's bus had left an hour ago and the two of them decided to catch a public bus from G.T. Road. Having stepped inside the tightly packed bus, they found to their dismay, that there was only standing space: they somehow managed to squeeze in and hold on to the railings. A man in his mid- twenties, wearing a red shirt, caressed Sara's cheek lovingly before swiftly alighting at the next stop. Disgusted, Sara ran down the steps and chased him, and hit him hard on his shoulder with her school bag. The startled man turned around to see her climbing up the bus steps; the driver had halted and was waiting for her. As she stepped inside and the bus began to move, there was loud clapping as the passengers applauded the gutsy girl who had dared to hit back at a man who had misbehaved with her. "Theek korecho!" cried an old lady approvingly, while an eldelrly man shouted "Bhalo korli!"

Renee wished she had her friend Sara's confidence in situations she faced in her own life. Her courage seemed to desert her when she needed it the most; deep insecurities emerged from within. She could never forget the humiliation she had to go through on the school stage while moderating a debate in class nine, two years earlier. Their school held regular debates among the students of classes nine, ten and eleven. The inter class debates were held in the large hall downstairs, and it was an event eagerly looked forward to by all the students of Classes six and above. Classes ten and eleven were going to debate the topic "Girls Should be Given as Much Freedom as Boys." Three girls from class eleven were going to argue for the motion and three from class ten were opposing it. The teachers required someone fluent in English, to introduce the topic and moderate the debate; Renee, a class nine student, was given the responsibility and their English Literature teacher trained her for it.

The debate was held in the large hall with students sitting on the floor and teachers on chairs placed along the sides. Six confident girls from senior school walked on to the stage and took their seats, three on each side. Sister Sophie sat on the extreme left, in front of the thick velvet, maroon curtains. Renee was waiting backstage with her English Literature teacher, Miss De Silva, who patted her shoulder and whispered, "Best of luck!" as she went up to the mike. She stared at the sea of faces in front of her, her mouth went dry and she could not utter a single word. Miss De Silva gestured frantically from behind the wings. "Say something, Renee!"

"I......" she began, "I......." She stopped speaking and stood there feeling ashamed.

The audience burst into laughter and her classmates looked at each other in shock and dismay. Sara wished she could run up and encourage her friend, Rita looked upset, and Cecilia stared at the ground.

Renee stood behind the mike, holding a piece of paper, unable to speak.

Sister Sophie rose from her chair and took the mike from Renee.

"I want all of you to stop laughing. Which one of you can

come up here on stage and speak? Tell me and come on up quickly." There was pin drop silence. She continued in a firm voice, "Renee's here on stage because she's better than any of you."

She turned towards Renee. "I know you can speak very well, child" she told her reassuringly, "Come, let's begin the debate…. Everyone's waiting."

Renee was no longer afraid. She felt safe and secure; her anxiety had disappeared. When she spoke on the mike her voice was loud and clear, her accent perfect, "Today the students of classes ten and eleven are going to argue the motion on the given topic. Let's hear them out and see for ourselves which side is more convincing. Before that let me introduce the participants…"

The girls in the hall clapped in appreciation and the teachers smiled in relief.

The academic year kept Renee occupied between her studies and many extracurricular activities. When she was studying in class ten preparations began for the Annual Concert sometime in the month of July. A dance teacher was engaged to teach them bhangra. He selected Renee and two of the taller girls in her class, as male dancers and the pretty, demure ones, including Sara, as the female dancers. It was a vigorous dance set to a catchy Hindi film tune; their teacher demonstrated each step and made them practice daily for almost half an hour. The boys were to wear lungis and kurtas with a head scarf tied around their heads; the girls were going to wear brightly coloured silk salwar kurtas.

Renee was horrified when her periods started the day before the concert. She did not tell her mother. In school that morning, she took Sara aside, "I've started..." she whispered in an anguished voice.

"Oh oh!" Sara threw back her head and laughed.

Renee scowled at her friend. "It's not funny," she said, "I'm scared. Suppose something happens."

"You silly girl," Sara replied confidently, "Nothing will happen. Just take extra precautions."

Renee's heart sank: she knew there was no backing out at this stage. On the afternoon of the concert, as they changed into their costumes in one of the empty classrooms, the girls chatted excitedly while Renee was unusually silent. She crossed her fingers and hope that everything would go off well. "Do well girls!" the dance master wished them, as the music started. The girls traipsed on to the stage from the left side of the wings, while the three male dancers came in from the other end. The loud music of the catchy tune reverberated through the hall and the girls danced vigorously. The audience, consisting of parents and siblings of the students, enjoyed their performance very much. Nothing untoward happened, and Renee heaved a sigh of relief as she changed her clothes to go home with her parents. Suddenly she felt a tap on her shoulder and she spun around to see it was Sara, grinning and giving her a thumbs up sign.

"All well?" she asked.

"Thankfully, yes," smiled Renee, as they left the room together.

In March of 1968, when Renee and her friends were studying in their Senior Cambridge class, preparations began for the

Annual Sports Day. The girls had a P.T. uniform, consisting of a white blouse and beige box-pleated divided skirt, to be worn twice a week for games with their sports teacher, the sprightly Mrs. Brown. In addition, it was mandatory for the students to wear white socks and canvas shoes.

Even as practice began in school, Renee had a major concern. While Mrs. Brown drove them relentlessly to practice all day in the sun, Renee had a secret worry: she was not sure if her mother would come to watch her. She wanted so much for *Mamoni* to be there, among the other parents on her big day. She began to have her doubts whether her mother would be able to attend; she had begun to notice how her mother seemed to lack the motivation to do anything on her own these days. She ran her household through Umer Singh, their bungalow peon, to whom she gave the daily menu and took accounts every evening. It was only occasionally that she decided to cook for her family and there was excitement all day as she busied herself in the kitchen. Renee watched fascinated as her mother made preparations to cook mutton do pyaza. She would mix the mutton with all the spices and curd in the right proportions; the sliced onions would be fried in mustard oil till golden brown and the mutton, some more sliced raw onion, and all the other ingredients would be added to it. The covered *dekchi* was placed on the coal "chulha" to simmer; as the slow cooking began, a delicious aroma filled the kitchen and the dining room. The taste was delicious when it was served with hot rotis for dinner that evening. There was similar anticipation when she baked the fish macaroni and cheese, in white sauce, in their small electric oven. She had learnt it during her stay in the United States and it became a family favorite as her children grew up. She would grate the cheese, debone the boiled fish, boil some macaroni, assemble the white sauce and mix it all together in a large baking dish. Renee watched intrigued as it was placed inside the warm oven. She would peep through the glass cover of the oven, from time to time, to watch the slow simmering as the top turned light brown. It was a grand occasion when *Mamoni* carried the browned pie dish to the dining table and father cut out the first slice. Renee felt the warm glow of togetherness as the family sat around the table for their evening meal and discussed the events of the day.

Whether or not her mother would be attending the Sports Day function was turning out to be a big worry for Renee. She wanted her mother to be present at her moment of glory, the team march past, for which they had been practising for weeks. When asked about it, *Mamoni* invariably looked disinterested and gave a vague reply. Her father would be coming, but that was not enough for Renee; what she yearned for was her mother's presence on the big day.

The school was brimming with activity on the morning of Sports Day. The gate had been painted afresh in dark grey and the durwan had a spanking new uniform for the occassion. The pathway to the open grounds was lined with potted plants on either side, adding a touch of greenery to the surroundings. The basketball court had been swept clean, and marked with red and white chalk, for the various events. The school staff was busy putting out folding chairs under the long, green tin shed, facing the sports field, where the parents and other guest would be sitting. The awards podium, which had been hauled out of the store room, dusted and cleaned, stood on one side of the sports field. A table, covered with an exquisitely embroidered table-cloth, was placed in front of the Principal's chair. Mrs. Brown and

Miss D'Silva arranged the glittering silver cups and medals in neat rows, placing the large team cup in the centre.

The parents had begun arriving from early morning and by ten o'clock most of the seats had been occupied. Sister Sophie came and sat in the front row, accompanied by Mrs. Ryan and Miss D'Silva. Class six students dressed in red and green T shirts and cream divided skirts took their positions, in neat rows of four to a line, for the first drill. A lilting tune filled the air as the music teacher began playing the recorded music; as if on cue, the girls raised their colourful hoops and began their drill. Their hand movements were perfectly sychronised and they bent their bodies gracefully in rhythm with the music. At the end of it, they marched off in single file, holding their hoops aloft to thunderous applause from the audience. Class seven students were already running on to the field holding green and yellow ribbons to begun their display. They waited patiently for the music to start, and at a whistle from Mrs. Brown began their exercise.

Renee looked anxiously at the gate; there was still no sign of her parents. Immediately after the drill display was over, it was time for the class races to start. There was immense excitement as the families cheered for their wards and shouted couragement to them to run faster and win a prize in the three legged race, sack race, or lemon and spoon race. The grand finale was the team march past, for which the students had been practicing for months. The girls made neat double lines as the Captains stood in front of them, proudly holding aloft the team flag, fluttering in the gentle breeze.   The martial music started and Sara was the first to lead her team, marching smartly in tandem to the drum beats. Shoulders up; arms and legs straight; left right, left right.

Renee followed with her Blue team; left right, left right. Her heart swelled with pride as she gave instructions in a clear and loud voice, her body ramrod straight, holding the blue colored flag aloft. "Baayein dekh!" she ordered, and all heads turned left towards the audience. Her spirits soared as she spotted *Mamoni* sitting beside her father and smiling. She had never felt so proud in her life. Her mother, along with others in the audience, was clapping and cheering as they marched past them. Later on in life, when things were not going her way, when there was no support from any quarter, Renee would see herself marching, holding aloft her beloved Blue team flag, and she would have no fear in the world.

The last few months of school were spent in completing the syllabus and preparing for their Senior Cambridge examinations which were to begin in the first week of November. Renee had been studying extra hours at home and had even stopped going out in the evenings to the Club as her exams approached. On the morning of their first paper, the girls huddled around the door of the large hall, where their exams were going to be held, pulling their sweaters tightly around themselves and doing last minute revision. Sister Sophie and Miss D'Silva were already inside and beckoned to them to enter exactly at nine o'clock. They went in and sat silently at their desks, while their teachers went around handing them answer sheets and the English Language question paper. All heads bent down as the girls started filling in their names and Roll numbers at the top of the answer sheet. Renee's mind went blank and try as she might, she could not remember her Roll number and began to panic. Beads of sweat appeared on her forehead as she raised her hand for help and Sister Sophie came over to inquire what the matter was. Renee heaved a sigh of relief when Sister gave her the Roll number, and she could finally begin writing her exams.

Sara came running up to her once they had handed in their answer sheets, and walked out into the corridor, on their way up to their classroom upstairs.

"What happened?" she asked in a concerned voice.

Renee smiled ruefully, "I messed up again...forgot my roll number!"

"*What!*" exclaimed Sara. "You did? What happened? I saw Sister Sophie near your desk..."

"Yes," Renee interrupted her, "I was so scared they'd throw me out of the examination hall. But Sister gave me the number immediately."

Sara laughed and pulled her friend's hand, "All's well that ends well. Come on, let's go and eat something." Together they went to get their lunch boxes from their bags and found their friends excitedly sharing their experiences of their first Board exam.

Once again, an inner insecurity had shown up in Renee's life, at the very moment when she needed to feel confident. She had hoped College and later, marriage would give her a sense of security but that was not the way things turned out to be. It needed someone like Kunal, who had weathered storms in his own youth, to make her feel safe again. He trusted no one because he had learnt early in life that people could be two faced, and the closest ones could betray you. He was careful to keep people he met at arms length and be wary of their overtures. He did not want any complications in his life, but they say the heart is a lonely hunter, and his resolve failed him once he met Renee. He never understood how she managed to enter the innermost spaces of his heart and make him love her so deeply. In doing so, she herself found the safety and security, she had yearned for all her life.

CHAPTER 6

RAJDEEP

Rajdeep lived with his parents, Rajeshwar and Sheila Varma, in a large house in Alipore Park Road. His grandfather had come to Calcutta from Bihar many years ago and started a small metal factory in the industrial area of Liluah, which made and supplied auto parts for Ambassador cars, manufactured by the Hind Motors Company in Uttarpara. Rajeshwar Varma had inherited the factory from his father and worked hard to make it prosper. He drove almost fifteen and a half kilometres daily by car to the factory in Liluah and spent the entire day there at his small site office which had three rooms, a washroom and a makeshift canteen. There was a patch of green grass within the premises, with a few potted plants, where he liked to sit in winter, in an old cane chair, and soak in the sun.

The Varmas had earlier lived in a rented apartment in Ballygunge, before moving to their own house in Alipore. Mr. Varma and his wife, Sheila, had lived on a tight budget all their lives and saved money; she had worked hard to bring up her three children, with only Bansi, the boy they had brought from their village, to help her with the household chores. The Varmas had a dream: they wanted to buy a beautiful house. Once every month they would drive to the prime localities of Calcutta, admiring the colonial bungalows. They had been saving for it for years and decided to search for one in the old Alipore area, with its mansions and stately houses built by the British, amidst a setting of verdant greenery. Alipore had large broad roads, lined with trees on either side: it was cool and shady to walk on the pavement in the summer months. Many consulates like those of Germany, France and Italy were located there, adding to the grandeur of the area. After independence, when the British began leaving the country, the locality became popular with the business elite, and a large number of them bought the bungalows and moved in.

One Sunday morning, the Varmas saw a 'FOR SALE' sign on the gate of a large bungalow on Alipore Park Road. It was a magnificent double storey house with a beautiful garden; Mr. Varma parked his car in the narrow road and went towards the white grill gate to make inquiries about it's price. Mrs. Varma had alighted and was now standing next to the car, admiring the house. Within five minutes she had reached a decision: this was going to be her new home. It's just right for us, she thought, the children are growing up, and we need more space. She immediately began gearing up for battle: she would need to use all her ingenuity to ensure her husband invested his money in a house of her choice.

An elderly caretaker, clad in a white dhoti and brown khadi kurta, came up and opened the lock of the gate to let them inside.

He greeted them with folded hands. "*Nomoshkar,*" he said.

"Namaskar," replied Mr. Varma. "Is this house up for sale?"

The man nodded. "Yes babu," he said, "You will need to contact the owner for more details."

Digging into his shirt pocket he brought out a small bundle of visiting cards, of which he handed one to him, asking him to contact the owner directly for further details. Mr. Varma thanked him and took the card, walking back briskly to his car. As they drove off, he expressed his fear to his wife that the price would be much above their reach. At least inquire, she urged him, you never know. She wanted this grand house for her own.

When Mr. Varma asked the owner it's price, he found it was way above their budget. "We'll have to let the house go," he told his wife that evening, "We'll start looking elsewhere, maybe Ballygunge itself or perhaps, New Alipore."

"Not at all," she replied, "I think the owner is asking a fair price."

"Where will we get the money?" he asked warily.

"Sell your share of the land in the village," she came straight to the point.

He was shocked. "Don't even think of it Sheila!" he shouted at her angrily. "It's my inherited property, and I intend keeping it. I am not going to sell it to buy you a house."

"Ashok and Rajdeep are not going back to the village to do farming," she replied calmly. "And Pinky will get married and go away to her in-laws' house."

Mr. Varma did not bother to reply and walked out of the room in a hurry, having remembered something urgent he had to attend to.

Mrs. Varma knew how to get her way around people, and it was true particularly in the case of her husband. She could be patient and scheming at the same time; it had been her life long strategy. She rarely let a day pass without raising the topic of the Alipore house. Her husband said nothing to her, but in fact, he had been thinking whether his sons Ashok and Rajdeep would be interested in going back to their ancestral village. He himself had moved to Calcutta with his parents many years ago. They had set up the factory in Liluah and all his friends and associates lived here. His children had grown up in the city and were now studying in good schools. If he decided to return, would they be able to adjust to life in a village? His thoughts began to veer around to his wife's suggestion that he should sell some of his inherited property and invest it in the house they had both liked.

Mr. Varma spent a week in his village selling enough land to raise money for the house he intended to buy in Calcutta. He finalized the deal with the owner and once the registration was done, took possession of the house. The bungalow on Alipore Park Road was repaired and painted a cream color, exactly the same as the other houses on the road. Each house had it's own unique architecture and gate; the small road running in the middle had a narrow cemented footpath on either side. The area was quiet during the daytime, after the menfolk left for work, and the children went to school and college. Occassionally hawkers, shouting out their wares made rounds, breaking the quiet of the surroundings.

The security guard of the Varma's house stayed in a room adjoining the large, iron grill gate; it had a window which opened on to the main road, from where he could look out for visitors. The driveway to the bungalow was paved with pebbles, to prevent formation of slush during the rainy season. There was a large porch with six steps leading up to a small landing, with green potted plants lining the entire length of the wall on both sides. The main door was made out of thick, polished teakwood with an ornate brass handle; a small window opened on the wall to the left and an exquisite, antique lamp hung on the right side. All the houses had boundary walls, three to four feet in height, with hedges planted alongside which had grown into thick, green foliage providing privacy to the residents. The entire area of Alipore was green with bushes and huge, shady trees spread all over.

The Varma family moved into their new home after performing a small puja on an auspicious day. The double storied house had a spacious open verandah at the back, overlooking a lawn with flower beds and a kitchen garden. The Varmas employed a full time *mali* who worked all day, pulling out weeds, watering plants, mowing the lawn, and did other sundry jobs. Very soon seasonal flowers bloomed in abundance and the garden was a myriad of bright colours, with the *mali* providing fresh flowers twice a week for Mrs. Varma to arrange in flower vases in the house. In winter, the vegetable garden provided carrots, radish, tomatoes, peas, chillies and coriander to the family kitchen and Bansi, the cook, made sure to include them in the day's menu, much to the delight of the children.

As one entered the house from the porch, there was a small corridor leading to the dining and drawing rooms. The Varmas had ordered some new furniture to fill the house, even as they spread out the stuff they owned in the different rooms. *Mr. Varma* had bought some beautiful pieces at one of the sales held regularly in the antique shops in Russel Street, one of which was the hat stand in the corridor, which combined utility with beauty: it had a rectangular mirror and ornate brass hooks on wooden panels on either side on which one could hang hats and topis. Below it, was a square wooden maze with empty slots to put umbrellas and walking sticks. In the centre were drawers for storing old newspapers and magazines; a tall flower vase with fresh flowers from their garden was placed on the small table top.

Straight ahead was the large drawing room, and to the immediate left, the spacious dining room. Mr. Varma had purchased an elegant glass cabinet, done in dark teak wood and the best Belgian glass and Ma had proudly displayed all the curios lovingly collected over the years. They included a long, silver boat in filigree work, a silver salver on a wooden stand, large sea shells, and a dancing figurine in delicate china. The rectangular centre table with a glass top, stood on a rich navy, red and beige carpet with an intricate pattern. A glass bowl of fresh flowers was placed in the middle; alongside were ash trays and carved glass and silver nut bowls. There was a radiogram in one corner with a tall lamp standing next to it; stacks of records, both in English and in Hindi, lay on a table close by.

Rajdeep and his elder brother Ashok studied in a boy's school in Kidderpore while their younger sister Pinky went to a girl's school close to it. Ashok was two inches shorter than Rajdeep and of stockier build; he enjoyed sports and was later in the College football team. On holidays he wore his shorts and tennis shoes and went for an early morning run around Alipore, while the city was still waking up. Pinky was of medium height, a little taller than her mother, and had a round pleasant face. Mr. Varma, whom the children called *Bauji*, was a humble man; there was an endearing quality about the way he treated each of his employees with the utmost respect, often sharing a cup of tea with them. On many a Sunday morning it was a familiar sight to see one of them turn up at his gate requesting a personal meeting. He would meet them in the small lobby where the hat-stand stood, while tea and biscuits were brought out. His advice was greatly valued by his employees. What outsiders were not aware of, was that *Bauji* had a controlling nature as far as his family was concerned. He had a strong, stubborn streak and expected everyone in the family to bow to his wishes. Rajdeep's mother, Mrs. Sheila Varma, however, proved to be an equal match for him. Over the years she had learnt that it was futile to argue with him; she could get her way around him, by sheer cunning and persistence.

With his sons, *Bauji* always wanted his point of view to prevail. His elder son Ashok simmered inwardly but said nothing. Their mother had a more adjusting nature and supported her children in all their endeavours; all she expected in return was their love and concern for her wellbeing. She directed all her energies to running her large household and was queen of her small kingdom. She drove the two house helps ceaselessly, faulting them for the smallest crease on the bedcover or the slightest speck of dust on the coffee table. In their struggle for survival the two of them, Birju and the ayah, had learnt to hoodwink her. They would disappear for short periods, each covering for the other. Their mistress would peer behind curtains and cupboards, shouting out their names for them to appear, so she could give them more work to do, but they would have fled temporarily. Bansi, the cook, who had originally come with them from their home state in Bihar, and had joined as a kitchen help, was her only ally. Under Mrs. Varma's expert tutelage he had graduated to full time cooking.

After finishing high school, Rajdeep joined the B.Com course in St. Xavier's College, Park Street. His elder brother, Ashok, was in the final year of a graduation course, in the same college. The family had assumed that after graduating from College, Ashok would assist *Bauji* in running the Liluah factory. It did not strike either of his parents to ask Ashok his own opinion about the matter. Rajdeep vividly recalled the morning in July, the day after his brother's results had been announced. He had passed with a good second division and Ma had sent the driver to buy *rasgullas* to celebrate. There was trouble the next morning when Mr. Rajeshwar Varma, bathed and ready in a crisp, white dhoti and kurta, came downstairs cheerfully for breakfast. Bansi had laid the table and placed the bread, butter and jam in the centre. As *Bauji* took his seat at the head of the table, Bansi brought in a steaming bowl of jeera aloo tamatar curry. Mrs. Varma came from the kitchen with two hot, golden fried puris and served both to her husband. He liked to eat a heavy breakfast before leaving for the factory; lunch consisted of fruits and a light snack from their canteen. Ashok walked in, looking dapper in dark trousers and a light blue shirt. He greeted his parents confidently and took his seat on one side of the dining table. Bansi appeared with his favourite double egg omelette stuffed with onion, tomato and dhaniya, fresh from their vegetable garden. Ashok buttered a toast, and placing half the omellete on top of it, carefully cut it into bite sized portions with his fork and knife. He ate his breakfast with great relish, savouring the taste of the fluffy, stuffed omellete and toast. Rajdeep, wearing jeans and a light coloured checked shirt, came in and joined them at the dining table. He had decided to go to College a little late that day and skip the first few classes; he wanted to see his brother accompany *Bauji* to the factory. Taking his seat, he quickly served himself some of the delicious aloo curry and took a hot puri. He asked Bansi to make him a fried egg. Mrs. Varma, and Pinky in her school dress, were the last to join them for breakfast.

Bauji and Ashok had finished eating by then and as if on cue, Bansi removed their plates and served them steaming cups of hot coffee. They drank in silence while the others ate. Mrs. Varma reminded her husband to buy fruits on his way back from Liluah; they were much cheaper in that part of the city than in Alipore. Ashok drank his coffee with studied indifference to their conversation. When everyone had finished eating, they rose to wash their hands, and Bansi came to clear the table. When *Bauji* went to fetch his briefcase from the drawing room he was surprised to find his elder son sitting on the sofa and reading the newspaper.

"Let's go Ashok," he said, turning towards the door.

"Where are you planning to go, *Bauji*?" inquired Ashok , nonchalantly.

Bauji spun around and replied quickly, "To the Liluah factory, of course. I want to introduce you to my Project Engineer and the rest of the staff as their new Sales Manager."

The effect was electric. Ashok was on his feet in a second.

"Excuse me *Bauji*," he said calmly, in a voice full of determination, "Can you please repeat what you said just now?"

There was stunned silence in the room.

"I said it's time for you to join the family business," his father replied in a firm voice.

"Time for me to join what *Bauji*? Your Liluah factory?" asked Ashok, staring defiantly at his father. "I am not going to drive up daily all the way to Liluah from here, in that awfully congested G.T. Road, which takes you almost an hour and a half to reach every morning."

Ma, Rajdeep and Pinky had overheard raised voices and came running in.

Mr. Varma was red with anger but he controlled his feelings, and replied in a steady and even voice, "As the elder son, it is your duty to carry forward the family business. I will not tolerate any other opinion in this matter. I have worked hard to provide all my children a life of comfort and I have the right to expect something in return."

"Oh I see! You have done us a great favour. And now I must repay, is that it?" asked Ashok, furious at what his father was implying.

His father's tone was uncompromising, "Yes, that's exactly what I meant. I am ashamed of having brought up such an ungrateful son."

"How can you speak so harshly to your own son?" cried Mrs. Varma, bursting into tears. Pinky clung to her mother's hand in fear.

Ashok paced up and down the room for a while. He stopped near the door and looked directly at his father. When he spoke his voice was strained, "So you are throwing charity at me, right *Bauji*?"

"Be reasonable, Ashok," his father said placatingly, "I am getting on in years. I find it very tiring to commute between

Liluah and Alipore every day. Besides, we must keep the factory going …..it's our bread and butter."

"There are other ways of earning an income….I am not going to work in your factory. Please understand that, *Bauji*," reiterated Ashok, "Don't waste your time trying to make me change my mind."

"My factory!" shouted *Bauji*. He turned to his wife. "You heard what your son just said ?" He looked so angry, she was afraid he would have a stroke or a heart attack.

"Please, please, calm down," she pleaded. "You will fall ill like this." She turned towards her son, "Be reasonable, Ashok... listen to what your father is saying."

Ashok was turning the door handle slowly. He had made up his mind. He was going to walk out of this house right now.

"You have run our lives till now," he said determinedly, "From now onwards, I am in charge of my own life."

"Then get the hell out of my house, you ungrateful bastard," shouted *Bauji*, in a voice full of hate and vitriol. Rajdeep was shocked to hear his father abuse his beloved brother. Mr. Varma had never raised his voice at either of his sons: they had been obedient boys. He had not had an inkling that Ashok wanted to live an independent life. He blamed himself for having spoilt his children and giving them all the luxuries they wanted, while he himself slaved it out in a far away factory . Exhausted, he slumped on to the sofa.

Ashok strode angrily out of the room. The servants had heard the commotion and gathered silently near the drawing room doorway. Rajdeep pushed aside Bansi in the corridor, and rushed behind his brother. He saw him stride across the gate, past the bewildered durwan and turn right towards the main road. Rajdeep ran outside and sprinted behind Ashok.

"Bhaiya! Stop!" he cried, catching up with him, and tugging at his shirt sleeve.

Ashok stopped, and giving him a hard look, roughly pushed him aside. "You stay out of this Rajdeep. I've had enough of *Bauji* and his imperious ways. He's not going to run my life any longer. " He continued walking briskly towards Alipore Park Road.

Rajdeep ran alongside his brother. "Don't listen to *Bauji*," he said imploringly. "Don't leave us, bhaiya! We need you."

Ashok had walked ahead and almost bumped into a hawker carrying a basket of fresh fruits on his head. A car came from behind, with their neighbour's College going daughters and honked loudly, asking for way. The brothers stepped aside. After the car had passed Ashok resumed striding ahead, Rajdeep trailing behind him. Desperately, he asked his brother not to do anything in haste. Matters could be sorted out, he told him. He need not go to the factory..... he could do something on his own, take up a job. Ashok was not listening. They had reached Alipore Park Road, where a yellow and black taxi was parked by the roadside, waiting to pick up passengers. Ashok opened the back door, sat inside and told the taxi driver, "Chalo. Fort William." He gave an address in the army cantonment. Rajdeep knew his brother's friend, who was a Captain in the army, lived there.

"Bhaiya!" Rajdeep cried, holding on to the taxi's open window, "Stay back!"

The driver had started the engine

"Rajdeep, you stay out of this!" shouted his brother, as the car began moving slowly.

Blinded by tears, Rajdeep stepped back, standing on the sidewalk until the taxi disappeared out of sight. He turned around forlornly and began the long walk back home. When he returned to the house his mother was standing in the porch crying, with Pinky by her side. *Bauji* was sitting in the car as Bansi put his briefcase and a thermos of hot tea on the seat beside him. Without speaking a word to anyone, he instructed the driver to take him to the Liluah factory. That evening Ashok's friend Shivender Singh rang up Rajdeep and informed him his brother was with him and not to worry.

Life went on as usual in the house on Alipore Park Road. Mr. Varma left for his factory in the morning and returned late in the evening. He felt tired by the end of the week, so he stopped going on Saturdays. He never mentioned the fracas with his elder son to anyone. He had accepted the situation with stoic calm and wished his son well in whatever he did. He hoped Rajdeep would give him support upon completing his graduation. He had been relieved to learn Ashok was well and had joined the Army. Mrs. Varma turned her attention to the upkeep of her house with renewed vigour. Pinky was in her final year in school and soon got absorbed in various activities and preparing for her board exams. It was not long before a smile was back on her face.

His elder brother's sudden departure affected Rajdeep deeply. Ashok bhaiya was his friend and companion, someone he looked up to for advice on the smallest of things. His brother always had an independent streak from childhood; he should have known, at some stage, he would rebel against their father's controlling nature. He wished he had had more time to talk things over with him and discuss their future plans but things had moved too fast that day. While walking back home that morning after Ashok left hurriedly in a taxi, Rajdeep suddenly grew up. He understood he would have to shoulder the family burden from then onwards. He would have to be careful not to hurt *Bauji* further and to make sure Ma did not feel neglected. He missed the carefree times with Ashok bhaiya in their bedroom, away from the prying eyes of their parents and Pinky's attempts at eavesdropping. There were times his brother returned home late in the night, after partying with his friends, and he would cover up for him. On other occassions he would be sleeping in late in the mornings, and his brother would lie to Ma that he was studying

"You take care!" Ashok bhaiya had always told him, and that was exactly what he intended to do. Rajdeep completed his B.Com and started accompanying his father to their auto parts factory in Liluah. He was greeted enthusiastically by all the staff and workers as their future boss. In the beginning he enjoyed the novelty of working: he looked up the financial ledgers, checked all the bills, and generally spent time on the shop floor. He brought in some changes too; he had the rickety furniture in the small canteen replaced by a new dining table and comfortable chairs. An air conditioner was installed so the employees could eat in a cool environment when the days were hot and humid. Yet the days were long and hard, and there was never any time for leisure activities. After about a year into this routine, Rajdeep began to realize that this was not the life he wanted to lead, spending his whole day in a factory far away from the bustle of a city.

Rajdeep was still in touch with his friends from St.Xavier's,

Park Street, from where he had graduated in commerce. Many of his classmates had joined British mercantile firms and Rajdeep was drawn to the glamour of their life. He admired their new sartorial elegance, the styling and stitching of their pin striped suits, the understated and matching ties they wore to work every day. He invariably joined his friends for Sunday outings to Park Street where they heard Louis Banks and Pam Crain and Usha Uthup live at Trincas. They ordered a round of drinks with cheese pakoras and fish fingers, and enjoyed each other's company in the invigorating ambience of the restaurant. Sometimes they drove to Nizam's for kathi rolls of their choice: mutton, chicken and egg wrapped in succulent parathas with crunchy raw onions soaked in lime juice. The place was invariably crowded with the well healed in their cars, ranging from Ambassador to Mercedes Benz, and the not so well off, in their hand rickshaws. The young men took in an occasional late night movie at the Globe or Elite cinemas or one of the grand English movie theatres. These had originally been drama theatres with ornate carvings on the walls of the stage, rich wooden paneling and maroon velvet curtains. Some still had quaint balconies, and bars, but now only screened the latest English movies.

Rajdeep realized he would have to find himself a job in a corporate firm, so he could fulfill his own aspirations in life. If he did not do so immediately, he saw himself going through the same daily grind he had seen his father go through. Ashok bhaiya had refused to be trapped in it and now he himself had begun to feel stifled; at the same time, he did not wish to hurt his father's feelings. He waited patiently for the right opportunity to broach the topic with *Bauji*. One Monday morning, as they drove up to Liluah in their Ambassador car, he spoke to his father, telling him that their auto parts business could be managed by employing a qualified Poject Manager.

Mr. Varma looked at him askance.

"Wait a minute...," he said, shocked. "Did I hear you correctly? You also want to leave the factory, like your elder brother?"

"No *Bauji*!" Rajdeep protested loudly. He paused, trying to sort out his thoughts. "I mean...Yes, I do," he admitted reluctantly. "Try to understand...There are so many opportunities open for me to find work and bring home a handsome salary."

His father shifted his position in the back seat to look at his son's face more closely. The car sped along the busy Strand Road weaving it's way through taxis, buses, hand carts and rickshaws. Soon they were crossing the majestic Howrah bridge. After a while, he shook his head and said in a bewildered voice, "I don't understand this at all."

"Nothing is wrong *Bauji*. It's just that I'm so bored at the sameness of things. There's so much else happening out there. Life can be so much more exciting than...," he stopped just in time, and bit his lip. He remembered his brother's defiant words. He did not wish to hurt his parents; whatever decision he took, he would have to keep their interest and happiness uppermost in his mind.

Mr. Varma sat back in his seat and took a deep breath. He felt defeated. He knew he would have to give Rjadeep the freedom to live his own life and make his own decisions.

"Tell me your plans," he said in a calm voice.

Rajdeep looked at him gratefully. He had been spared the fierce battle he had anticipated with *Bauji*. It was almost four years since Ashok bhaiya had left home and *Bauji* had mellowed with age, letting others in the house make their own decisions. Time changes everyone.

Rajdeep had applied for the job of Executive Assistant in one of the top tea companies which exported tea from Calcutta. He was thrilled when he received his appointment letter within days of giving an interview with the Managing Director. His new office was in a multi- storied building on Chowringhee Road. The relatively short journey from Alipore Park Road to his office was a big relief for Rajdeep, after the daily morning battle to reach their factory. From the first day itself, he enjoyed the buzz of his new work place. There were challenges to be met everyday and he worked with smart young men his own age, from whom he learnt a lot. One of them told him about Lakeview Club in the Railway Colony in Alipore. They had recently opened up membership to outsiders and Rajdeep decided to apply, as it was close to his house. He wanted to start playing tennis again, a game he had enjoyed in College. Once his membership was granted he began going regularly. After a strenuous game, he liked to cool down with a cold drink and one evening he saw a pretty girl walk quietly in, and sit on a cane chair to read the latest issue of Filmfare magazine.

CHAPTER 7

KUNAL

Renee had first seen Kunal Chopra while she had been sitting with Rajdeep during the fete at the Lakeview Club. She was unaware that he had recently joined the Club as a private member. She had noticed his intelligent look and his self-confidence, and the self assured way in which he carried himself. Kunal was conservative in his choice of clothes; his one indulgence were the blue jeans he liked wearing on Sundays in his hostel in IIT, Kanpur. He enjoyed the sense of freedom it gave him. When he started working in Calcutta he went to work in dark trousers and white or pastel colored shirts, as was the norm in the 1970's. He made sure to polish his shoes till they shone and liked wearing socks in light checks or self -design. They matched the color of the tie or shirt he was wearing that day. After the extreme cold weather of Lucknow, he found the winters in Calcutta mild and liked to mostly wear his favourite navy blue blazer.

Kunal worked in the Marketing and Sales division of a well known Steel Company which had it's office on Chowringhee Road. He had rented a small apartment in Block E, New Alipore and because it was South facing there was always a pleasant breeze in the evenings. The Bengali family who owned the house lived on the ground floor, and had divided the upper portion into two small flats which had been rented out, the other occupant being a young man from Madras who worked in India Tobbaco Company. New Alipore was one of the better planned residential areas of Calcutta and was cosmopolitan in it's character. A wide variety of people from all over the country lived here. The neighbourhoods had paved sidewalks, lined with trees and, in addition, there was adequate street lighting. It was well connected by public transport to various parts of the city. Kunal took a bus to work every morning, preferring to hire a taxi on the way back, when he was tired and in a hurry to reach home. He had hired some furniture from a shop close by: a bed with side table, a wooden cupboard and a study table with chair. He had bought a fridge, an electric kettle and a small, electric heater to cook food. He was able to get by on his diet of tea, coffee, cornflakes, omellete and fruits. A toaster he had picked up in New Market had been added to his kitchen. Lunch was at the office cafeteria; it was amusing to watch the trainees and young officers pile their plates high with chicken biryani, while the calorie conscious senior men, made do with soups and salads.

Kunal's father, Kishan Chand Chopra, worked in one of the departments of the Central government, and the family had move around in various towns in Northern India, due to his frequent transfers. Kunal's brother Sunil was two years younger to him, and almost the same height as him. Youngest was sister Ragini, as talented and attractive as their mother. His mother, Kamla Chopra, was a homemaker, completely devoted to the welfare of her family. She enjoyed cooking for them and spent the winter months knitting sweaters for various members of her family. She had been a beautiful young woman and had aged with grace and dignity. Life's blows had not succeeded in touching her steely resolve to do the best for her children and she had always been a great source of strength to them.

When Kunal was studying in class seven his father got posted in a department in Lucknow. They lived in a bungalow in a residential colony meant exclusively for government officers. It had wide, tree lined roads and each house had a well maintained lush, green lawn with seasonal flowers in bloom and potted plants lining the small driveway. Raw mangoes hung tantalisingly from trees in the summer months and the *mali's* and other kids had a grand time picking the ones which fell to the ground during the frequent dust storms. The family got to eat some ripened ones too, and they were delicious dussehri mangoes. The gulmohar trees blossomed in the brightest orange and red when in season.

While studying in the Senior Cambridge class, Kunal began attending tuition classes for the Indian Institute of Technology entrance exams. After their final exams were over in November 1963, while their other friends vacationed, Kunal along with four other boys, continued studying at home. The tests were held in the third week of April and although Kunal had done his best he was not sure how he would fare. When the results were declared in early June, he was thrilled to see his and another friend's name on the list of successful candidates. After paying the fees, he was called to the IIT Kanpur campus, along with his father, for counselling sessions. He was lucky to get the stream of his choice, mechanical engineering.

Even as Kunal was excited about joining the engineering course, a deep fear struck his heart, as he bent down to touch his father's feet and seek his blessings, before leaving for his hostel in Kanpur. His father, Kishan Chand Chopra, was living on borrowed time. Kunal had been all of eleven years old, studying in class five, when he had accidently overheard, the devastating news of his father's grave illness. He had been happily walking to his mother's bedroom, when he suddenly stopped behind the slightly open door. He could hear her crying. Quietly, he peered inside. She was sitting on the bed sobbing, his father seated next to her, with his arms around her shoulders.

"What will I do…," she wept, "If anything should happen to you? The children are so young…"

"Don't worry Kamla. Wahe Guruji will take care of everything. I have an appointment with the cancer specialist at Tata Memorial Hospital in Mumbai next week. My department is making all the arrangements. I have a flight ticket for next Sunday."

"Cancer of the throat!" she cried, "You know it's not curable."

"Not anymore," he replied in a calm voice. "Medical science has advanced a lot these days: there's chemotherapy and radiation in addition to medicines. The Doctor says with proper treatment I can make full recovery. That is why he is sending me to the best hospital in the country. We have to be strong, Kamla…the children must not be told about my illness. They will worry and be scared."

Kunal stood rooted to the spot. He stepped back behind the blue printed curtain; he knew he should not be eavesdropping, that it was wrong to be doing so. Yet, his feet were paralysed. He stood there and strained his ears to listen.

"I'll tell the children I'm going to Bombay on official work," he continued.

"How can you hide such a grave illness from them?" his wife protested. "They will know something is very wrong."

"On my return I'll tell them I'm not well and undergoing treatment."

Kunal felt sick in his stomach. He thought he was going to vomit. His beautiful, secure world was shattered in one moment. What of his school? What if his father should die? Would he have to stop studying? The questions came thick and fast. Kunal swallowed the pill of fear and it went and lodged itself deep inside, somewhere between his heart and the pit of his stomach. It was like one of those bright orange capsules, his father had lately begun taking. It stayed inside him, even as he grew into manhood, and learnt to face the harsh realities of the world. It would need a woman's deep love to free him of the pain. He had no idea if such a thing was at all possible and no idea, where he would meet a woman who was meant to love him either.

He watched his father from behind the curtain. He was holding his mother's hand gently and reassuring her, "You are a brave woman, Kamla. We have been through so much together and you have always stood by my side. I promise you everything will be fine. Have faith in God."

"You have never done anything wrong," she whispered agonizingly, "Why us?"

"He tests even the best of us," Kishan Chopra spoke in a calm voice. "Even when I'm not here, I'll be watching over you and the children, every moment . You know that."

She put her hand up to his lips and admonished her husband, *"Shubh shubh bolo ji! Aap treatment waste tyaari karo. Main sab sambhal loongi."*

Kunal walked away and told no one about his father's illness. In class, he would look furtively at his happy friends, laughing and joking, and making a ruckus in the classroom in their teacher's absence, and wonder if all this was going to end for him anytime soon. He began to be careful about how he spent his pocket money; he focused on his studies. He helped his mother around the house. When his father went away on long leave to Bombay for treatment and later, for follow ups, at the Tata Memorial Hospital, he became the man of the house. He stopped fighting with Sunil over small things and helped Ragini with her school work. He grew up overnight. His father made a complete recovery and the Doctors in Bombay assured him the disease was in remission. He rejoined work and peace and joy returned to the Chopra household. His mother went about her work looking serene and happy as before.

Into his third year in the B.Tech course, Kunal got a late night trunk call from his mother in Lucknow. He had not been home for almost two months, busy as he had been, preparing for his fourth semester examinations. He knew his father had not been keeping well and had been to see his General Physician, who had advised various investigations to identify the problem. That night Mama had come straight to the point. *Papa's* old disease was back, she said. When his father had returned from his first round of treatment at Tata Memorial Hospital, Bombay, the Doctors had warned him that in case the illness appeared again, there was little they would be able to do about it.

Kunal's heart was heavy when he boarded the bus for Lucknow early next morning. A few kilometres out of Kanpur, the bus stopped for a tea break for the passengers. Kunal got down with many of the others and gulped a cup of sweet, milky chai. He paced up and down restlessly till it was time to board the bus again. After this visit, Kunal made frequent trips home and each time, he noticed how weak his father looked. The treatment had begun in earnest, but this time it did him no good. It was heartbreaking to watch him go and be able to do nothing about it. Within a few months, his father passed away. Mrs. Kamla Chopra showed stoic calm through all of this. She knew she had to be strong for her children's sake; she was determined to give them the best start she possibly could in life. Their future lay ahead and she wanted them to lay solid foundations with hard work and grit. The family vacated the government bungalow and shifted to rented accomodation in the Mahanagar locality of Lucknow. Sunil was studying in first year of College and Ragini was in High School. Kunal returned to IIT, Kanpur to complete his engineering course.

CHAPTER 8
YOUNG AND FREE

When the Senior Cambridge results were finally announced, sometime in March of 1968, Renee was thrilled to find she had passed with a high first division. Her father had been transferred to Lucknow and she studied and completed her graduation in English (Honours) from a College there. Mr. Srivastava was posted in the Research Designs and Standards Organisation in Manaknagar in Alambagh. The railways had acquired large tracts of land belonging to adjacent villages and developed the area into a full fledged residential cum office colony. Renee and her family lived in a brick colored bungalow built almost like the barracks, in that, it was elongated in shape, with all the rooms side by side, and only the dining room and kitchen towards the back.

There was a large patch of lawn in front; small evergreen plants grew along it's edges, which had a neat looking border of slanting bricks. There were two gates, one on the extreme left, and the other on the right side, which lead to the main road connecting the Railway Colony to Alambagh. When Renee joined College, her brothers Jatin and Sonu, were admitted to a boys school in the city. Her College was far from the colony, and she comutted by public bus. She went to Alambagh by rickshaw every morning and then took the bus to the city. She liked to sit by the window inside the bus, watching the city go by: first Kaiserbagh, past the Charbagh Railway station, then the Odeon cinema with posters of the latest Hindi movies, past the grand building of the Vidhan Sabha to the right and finally the bus taking the left turn towards Hazratganj. The bus drove over the Gomti bridge, went past the Lucknow University and reached her College. She had joined the English (Honours) course and worked hard at her studies.

She had begun her third year in B.A. when her father returned home from office one evening and made a surprise announcement. "I've been transferred," he told his wife and daughter , even as he ate *a salty snack* from a *katori* and sipped his tea.

"Again!" cried Renee, "What of my college?"

Years of frequent transfers had prepared her mother for such news. She asked her husband calmly, "Where to?"

He replied quickly, "Back to Calcutta…..I have been posted at the head office in Fairlie Place."

Renee could not believe what she was hearing. Another transfer!

"I can't give up my B.A. in my final year," she said, feeling upset.

"You don't have to," said her father firmly, "You can move into the girls hostel in your College."

"No way!" cried Renee, "I've never lived away from home. I am not going to do that." She had visions of dirty laundry, hard wooden beds, tinda and turnip curry with leathery chappatis for dinner.

There was silence for a few minutes as Umer Singh came and took away the tea tray. Their argument continued for a while till she understood there was no other option open to her.

She reluctantly applied for a seat in the hostel; she was granted one without fuss, the fees were paid and the formalities completed within a week. The packing of all the furniture and other stuff in their house had started, so they could be loaded on a train wagon and sent to Calcutta. She packed her toiletries, clothes, books and other essentials in a tin trunk, feeling sorry for herself; she knew she would miss *Mamoni's* pampering. She was afraid too; she was going to have to adjust to a harsher life. In the event, things turned out better than she had anticipated. For one thing the food was good, she made friends quickly with the other girls who stayed in the hostel and very soon she began enjoying her new life. Saturdays were eagerly looked forward to, for it meant the girls could go out to Hazratgunj for an outing. There was something about "gunjing"_she remembered eating her first burger at Modern Novelties. In all her later travels, Renee would never eat anything so good; it consisted of a fresh oven baked bun stuffed with an Amul cheese cube and topped with dollops of tomato ketchup. Then a cup of Espresso coffee at the kiosk outside, which played, *"Yahoo yahoo! Chahe koi mujhe junglee kahe….."* at full volume. Boys would be casting admiring glances at the pretty girls, the bolder ones commenting, *"Ama yaar, kya cheez hai."* The girls would not take offence, rather bask in the praise, and walk off with a toss of their heads and sway of their dainty hips. It was all done in good humour and it was harmless fun. Renee and her friends would shop at Halwasiya Market, eat lunch and then catch the bus back to College, and return just in time to beat the evening curfew.

Renee completed her classes and appeared for her Third Year final examinations in the month of May in 1971. She vacated her hostel room and left for her parents' new home in Calcutta. Another transfer. Another beginning.

Kunal completed his B. Tech.in Mechanical engineering in 1967 and began applying for jobs. Within a month he got selected to work in the Marketing and Sales division of a well known steel company which had its Sales head office on Chowringhee Road in Calcutta. This was a brand which had built up trust and respect over the years and that was the reason he was elated at being able to work with them. The city had so much to offer a newcomer like him. It enveloped him in its warmth amidst all the daily chaos, traffic jams, teeming hordes and the sweet joy of eating syrupy *roshogollas* and *mishti doi*. The spirit and bonhomie among the people was infectious. It was possible to lead a good life regardless of the size of one's wallet: one could enjoy street food and steal a late night show in one of the grand cinema halls like Metro or Elite. Kunal discovered that Calcutta had a rich Club life; very few cities offered a greater variety. Along with a few of his colleagues he entered the Merchants Cup tournament and played some mediocre cricket learnt in school. That was totally beside the point. The important thing was the fellowship and spirit of carmaderie it generated, along with a banquet of fine wines and sumptuous food. Kunal particularly liked the Tollygunge Club which had a green and vastly spread out golf course where enthusiastic golfers could be seeing teeing off in the mornings and afternoons, their loyal caddies, with their golf sets in tow. Besides,the lush green lawns and numerous shady trees provided a breath of fresh air among the teeming crowds, which seemed to be everywhere he went. He decided he would apply for corporate membership sometime in the future when he was more financially secure.

Even as he started his new life in Calcutta, Kunal would often think of his family back in Lucknow. He appreciated his mother's struggle to keep the family together. His younger brother Sunil was preparing for the competitive examinations after completing his post-graduation in History. Ragini was doing her graduation course and growing up into a well-mannered, responsible girl. He was very cautious about money matters, sending home part of his salary to his mother every month. After almost four years of service, he decided he could afford to join a Club and applied for membership in April 1971, to the one nearest to his house, the Lakeview Club. Kunal would take a taxi to the Club to while away a few hours in the evening over the weekend.

Around the month of June, he was drinking a Coca Cola, and trying to concentrate on reading the latest issue of Time magazine when he saw an attractive young girl dressed in a pink churidar kurta, her lustrous mid length hair tied loosely, walking towards the main building. She was slim and he saw she had a good figure. She turned to settle her hair as the gentle South breeze played with the unwieldy strands and he noticed how soft and gentle her expression was. Renee walked straight up to her father who was speaking to Rajdeep. As he watched her from a distance, he was struck by her confident and self assured bearing.

After completing her graduation from Lucknow, Renee had joined her parents in Lakeview Park. Many of her College friends had got married and begun an exciting new journey in their lives. Her brothers Jatin and Sonu were still completing their studies. She had yet to make up her mind about joining a post graduate course and for the time being, was enjoying her break. While she spent her days reading books and staying at home with *Mamoni*, in the evenings she stepped out, looking for friends her age, which was hard to find in the gated colony, as most of the children were away studying in other cities. She would invariably go to the Railway Club for her favourite cold drink and potato wafers. She often saw Rajdeep there on weekends, playing tennis, but they hardly ever spoke. One Saturday, while she was sitting in the Club verandah, he joined her after his game of tennis and surprised her by asking if she would like to accompany him to Trincas restaraunt the next evening for a jam session. In the sixties and seventies, Park Street was the hot spot of entertainment: live rock and jazz was played in restaurants like Blue Fox and Moulin Rouge but it was Trincas which was the favourite of the young and swinging crowd. It introduced band music and had many immensely popular singers, including the legendry Usha Uthup, who sang in her melodious throaty voice many evenings.

Renee was immediately excited at the idea; she had heard so much about Trincas that she wanted to accept Rajdeep's invitation. However, there was one major problem: she would need to get her parents permission. When she broached the subject over dinner that night, her mother flatly refused.

Mamoni almost choked over her roti and aloo gobi curry. "Go out with another man! Before marriage. Absolutely out of the question. What will people say?"

An argument ensued between mother and daughter. Renee insisted it was only for a few hours and *Mamoni* should see nothing more to it.

"Girls from our family don't go out with strange men," her mother was adamant.

Her father had to intervene and assure his wife that he knew Rajdeep personally and that he came from a good family. Her mother felt strongly that Renee should not go; in her opinion, girls went out only with the man they were married to. She was aware, however, that times were changing and she knew she would have to change with it. Reluctantly, she agreed, provided Renee returned before dinner time.

The next evening Renee was dressed and waiting eagerly for Rajdeep, even as her mother looked on disapprovingly. She was excited about visiting Trincas; as a teenager, she had longed to enter it, and peeped in furtively, while walking past with her parents when they came for lunch to Kwality restaurant from Liluah. Rajdeep arrived promptly at six, parked his car in their porch and rang the doorbell. Her father opened the door and greeted him warmly; her mother said nothing. Once they were seated in the car, Rajdeep started the engine and they sped away. It being Sunday, the traffic was sparse, and soon they were driving past the Race Course, towards the Maidan.

In Park Street, Rajdeep found parking space a little ahead of Trincas, and the two of them joined the eager, jostling crowd of youngsters inside the restaurant. The boys and girls teeming inside were young and free: the world belonged to them and they wanted to celebrate it. Inside Trincas, a live band was playing; Renee instantly recognized them as The Cavaliers, immensely popular those days, for the new sounds they were introducing. The dance floor was full of young couples energetically gyrating to the rhythmic music and the air throbbed with sound and lights. Renee had been eager to come, but once inside, she began to feel out of place, and was grateful when Rajdeep steered her quickly towards an empty table with two cane chairs. They took their seats and soon a waiter appeared and they ordered cold drinks, potato chips and cheese pakoras.

Renee stared wide eyed at the couples dancing with so much grace and energy, and before long she had relaxed and begun to enjoy the ambience and the heady noise. Rajdeep was glad to see that she was smiling and tapping her feet to the rhythmic beats. Once they had eaten, they decided to leave. It was dark by the time they came outside and the bright, multicolored neon lights of the shops and restaurants had been switched on. Park Street looked like a fairyland with bejewelled sign boards and the sidewalk teeming with people; the atmosphere was electric. It had become cool and the two of them made their way to their parked car, a little distance away. On the way back, Rajdeep asked Renee if she had enjoyed the outing.

"Yes, I did. Thank you very much!" she replied.

He dropped her to her house, said goodbye and drove off. Renee went inside and was grateful to be enveloped in its secure warmth Renee had been enjoying her holidays since she had come to Lakeview Park after completing her graduation from Lucknow. It was already the beginning of August when she noticed a buzz among the officer's wives. On inquiring from her father at home one evening she discovered that their ladies Club was organizing it's Annual Fete on the Club lawns. Renee looked forward to attending it and hoped she would like the fun and games.The fete was held in the middle of August and the day dawned bright and clear, sparing the organizers the worry that it might rain in the evening.

It being a Saturday, Kunal decided to visit the fete being held at the Lakeview Club. He took a taxi and alighted at Alipore Road, preferring to walk the rest of the way. He deftly manouvered his way through the crowd, bought some coupons at the entrance stall and went in. He wanted to eat something and asked for two hot, vegetable patties served with tomato ketchup. Having finished these, he went to the Espresso stall and paid for a cup of steaming coffee. He took a sip and as he looked around the holiday crowd enjoying themselves, he saw Renee talking animatedly to Rajdeep. She was looking beautiful in a light mauve colored sari, with the make up she had put adding a glow to her face. It was the first time he had seen Renee wear a sari and he liked the way it flowed over her rounded hips. He looked away, turning his attention to one of the games stalls.

Kunal pulled up a chair at some distance. He could see Renee from where he sat, and observed how she looked a mixture of vulnerability and self-assurance. She seemed an intelligent and confident girl, whom he would have liked to know better. He noticed his staring had angered her, and she had turned her face away from him. He laughed softly to himself: so she could be vain and haughty too, qualities which were sure to land a young woman in trouble. He shook himself from his reverie, and remembered his family responsibilities. His sister Ragini had completed her graduation and some of their relatives in Lucknow were already suggesting eligible bachelors to his mother, who wrote long letters to him discussing each proposal in detail. He knew his sister had to be married first, before he could even think of settling down.

His brother Sunil had begun working and was financially independent and took care of Mama. He decided to leave and strode briskly towards the main gate of the colony to get a taxi and go home.

A few days later, Renee had a massive argument with her father. Back from office one evening, he asked her to start preparing for the Indian Civil Service examinations. She had been excellent in her studies and participated in many extra-curricular activities in school and college and he felt she had a fair chance of succeeding in the tough exams.

Renee stared at him aghast. "*Papa!*" she cried, "Since when did you decide you could plan my future?"

His reply was quick, "I am only suggesting the right thing to do for a bright student like you."

"I don't wish to work," she replied decisively. "I am sure of one thing…. I don't want a career."

Her father spoke calmly, "We're looking around for a suitable boy from a good family for you, Renee. In the meantime, the preparation would keep you busy, instead of sitting idle all day."

Renee responded sharply, "What's the point of it when I'm not interested in a job?"

Her mother looked at her daughter disapprovingly. "Don't be rude to your father," she admonished her. "He means well for you."

Her father shrugged his shoulders, "She's wasting her time…"

"*Papa!*" protested Renee, pushing her chair back and standing up, "Please try to understand, I don't want a career."

She had visions of herself slaving in a nondescript office, working from morning to evening, leading a colourless life. Worse! What if no man found her appealing enough to marry her?

"I think I'll take a walk," she said, walking towards the porch, "It's cool outside."

In fact, Renee's parents had been searching for a suitable boy for their daughter ever since she completed her graduation. Mr. Srivastava had sent a formal proposal, along with her photograph, to a few families and entered into correspondence on this matter with them. Nothing had materialized so far; some demanded hefty cash amounts, others asked for expensive gifts and an extravagant wedding. Renee's father was wary of such people for he was well aware that his own resources were limited. He had met Rajdeep Varma and liked him. He was a polite, well behaved boy and came from a financially sound family and seemed just the kind of groom they were searching for Renee. He decided to discuss the matter with his wife in a few days. The very next morning, some urgent work came up in office and he had to leave Calcutta for a week's tour.

Chapter 9

Longings Of The Heart

In spite of her vehement argument with her father, it was very boring for Renee to sit at home all day. She had been used to the hectic schedule of school and college, filled with extra-curricular activities, and the joyous company of her friends. Now the days stretched long and endlessly. Reading was her only solace, and she found she had read through all the books at home. The next day, even though her father had gone out of Calcutta on tour, she decided to take a taxi and go to Oxford Book Store on Park Street to buy a few books. *Mamoni* gave her money and told her to make sure she returned soon. She wore her jeans and a light blue top and putting on her sneakers, she picked up her purse and walked briskly towards the main gate. It was only the second time she was venturing out of Lakeview Park on her own, the first being when she had gone by cab to New Market when she needed to buy some things. An empty taxi finally appeared and when it stopped, she sat in the back seat and gave the driver her destination. They cruised at a steady speed on the tree lined, smooth road, past the Race Course, turning right towards the Nehru Planetarium. It being early evening, there was light traffic but she could see dark clouds moving speedily towards the city from across the Bay of Bengal.

They reached Park Street and she asked to be dropped near Oxford Book Store, where she paid and got off.

Once inside the shop, she walked to the fiction area where books were stacked in racks, according to author, name and genre. She was surprised to see Kunal bending down on his knees and searching among the various titles. So he was fond of reading, too; he must have left office early, to pick up a book before returning to his New Alipore flat. They had been introduced a few days earlier by Rajdeep. She was curious to know his favourite authors; she saw he was holding The Grapes of Wrath by John Steinbeck. She wanted to read Rebecca by Daphne du Maurier and searched for it. The salesman standing close by informed her that they were out of stock at the moment. She decided to buy Airport by Arthur Hailey, instead. Kunal and Renee reached the billing counter together and he stepped aside, to let her pay. Clutching her purse and packet, she hastily stepped outside to get a taxi and go home, only to find that it was raining heavily by now. As she stood under the awning, Kunal came out and walked ahead; he was back in a few minutes to find her still standing there, waiting for a taxi to appear.

"How will you go home?" he asked, "Is someone coming to pick you up?"

Heavy rain lashed the railings and she stepped back.

"No," she shook her head, "My father is away on tour. I came alone."

She held her arms close and shivered. Many people had taken shelter on the broad sidewalk. A buxom, middle aged lady, holding an umbrella jostled for space and pushed Kunal, admonishing him, "Amake dhakka dichcho kyano?" (Why are you pushing me?")

Kunal moved closer to Renee. She could smell his cologne and powder and sweat: it was a heady mixture and his male smell made her feel safe. She stopped shivering.

"I'll drop you home," he said hurriedly. "Let me get a taxi first."

As he went to the edge of the road a car sped by, splashing muddy water all over his trousers and shoes. He laughed ruefully. The water had begun collecting in the low lying areas, on either side of the road. Cars and taxis carrying passengers sped past as they waited. Regulars knew how difficult it was to get home from office on a rainy evening; one could be stuck in a massive traffic jam for hours, if the roads got flooded. Sometimes one simply had to fold one's trousers and wade through or one could sit aloft one of the hand pulled rickshaws, which could negotiate the trickiest of lanes. Kunal looked at his watch: six thirty and already dark. To his great relief a taxi slowed near them, and they climbed in.

"Alipore," Kunal directed the driver.

"You're drenched!" exclaimed Renee. He pulled out his handkerchief and wiped his face and hair. As their cab drove by Park Street, Renee peered out of the window, and saw the neon lights flickering on the signboards of restaurants and shops, and the street lights glowing like jewels. She lowered the window pane, and felt a rush of cool air caress her face. They drove on in silence and turned left towards Nehru Planetarium. The car slowed down at the roundabout, where there was complete chaos, each driver trying to outsmart the other. Horns were blaring and it was a free for all, when a traffic policeman suddenly appeared, and began directing the traffic.

Kunal turned towards Renee. "What do you plan to do after finishing your studies?" he inquired.

"I haven't thought of anything yet," she replied. The taxi had turned left, and much to everyone's relief there was less traffic on the wide road and they drove at a steady speed.

"You can afford to wait," he retorted, "Women don't have the responsibility of earning the bread and butter. You can work for the jam."

She glared at him.

"I know!" he laughed, "That was a very rude thing to say."

They were getting close to Lakeview Park. All at once the taxi began jolting with a loud thudding noise, dragged on for a few meters and came to a sudden halt. The driver got off and walked around checking all the tyres of the taxi.

He stopped near Kunal's open window at the back. "Flat tyre," he announced. Thankfully, it had stopped raining and the two of them alighted and Kunal paid the driver. They decided to walk back to Lakeview Park, as it was less than a kilometer away.

On their way they saw a small tea stall, the kind that had a saucepan boiling with hot, sweet tea at all times of the day. Kunal wanted to stop for tea and they ordered two cups and after he had paid, took the steaming "kulhars" from the stall owner gratefully. They sipped the sweet, milky tea with the aroma of cardamom and felt the warmth soak into their chilled bodies. They finished their tea and started walking towards Lakeview Park. The sidewalk was wet after the rain, and muddy water had collected at many places; she stopped at a particularly large puddle, staring at it with trepidation. Kunal saw her hesitate, and stretching out his hand, held hers in a firm grip, and helped her jump across. At his touch, she felt a magnetic pull, almost as though she would be unable to let it go. Hastily she pulled her hand away, and continued walking in silence. Renee was confused: she thought she disliked Kunal's arrogance; his confident bearing. Yet, almost against her own will, she was attracted towards him! Walking beside him, she felt calm and contented, as if she had always known him and could trust him. He walked ahead fast, without waiting for her, and she had to almost run to keep up with him.

Abruptly, he stopped, and turned around, "You shouldn't have come out in this weather."

"I didn't know it was going to rain!" she protested. He had resumed striding and she ran behind, trying to catch up with him.

They entered the main gate of the railway colony, lit up by street lights. Soon they had reached her house, and Renee ran lightly up the steps and rang the doorbell. He bade her goodbye and left for home.

As he traced his steps back towards Alipore Road, Kunal realized he was walking away from the one girl he felt drawn to, in a world in which he had faced rejections from so many quarters. He sensed a caring tenderness in Renee, like a balm to the wounds he still carried deep inside him. He himself felt protective towards her, as if he wanted to save her from the buffets of life. No words were spoken but each felt complete in the other's presence; he wished he could get to know her better. He also realized her parents would be looking to find a suitable match for her, whereas he himself had responsibilities towards his own family. He hoped a girl like Renee would find happiness where ever her destiny took her.

Next Sunday evening, as Renee was leaving the Railway Officers' Club, she bumped into Kunal.

"Hello!" he greeted her, "Leaving early today?"

"Yes," she replied, "We're having some people over for dinner."

He stood looking at her for a moment. "Do you like *golguppas*?" he asked abruptly.

"Why yes, I do!" she replied, taken by surprise.

"Then meet me tomorrow at the Maidan, opposite the Victoria Memorial gates..."

"...but you have office," she interrupted him quickly.

"I'll work during lunch time and take a short break at four thirty in the evening. I'll walk over from my office and meet you...it's close by, on Chowringhee Road. Be there," he said, and strode off towards the Club building.

Renee stared at him. Was he ordering her to meet him? Well, she would think about it, she decided, and not necessarily follow his instructions.

Next afternoon, she was all fidgety, trying to think up excuses to get her mother's permission. She could not possibly tell her she was going to meet a young man on her own.

At lunch that day, she broached the topic. "*Mamoni,*" she asked hesitantly, "Can I go to the Chowringhee arcade at four this evening?"

"Why, what's the matter? What work do you have there?" inquired her mother, looking up from her plate.

"A friend of mine from Lucknow is visiting Calcutta and has asked me to meet her there."

Her mother looked at her daughter doubtfully.

"Are you sure you want to go alone?"

"Yes," Renee nodded emphatically.

"Be sure to be back early," her mother reluctantly gave her permission.

Renee was dressed and out of the house promptly at four that evening. She pulled the porch door quietly shut behind her, and walked briskly to the main gate of their colony. An empty taxi was cruising slowly, looking to pick up passengers, and she waved to him to stop.

"Victoria Memorial," she said, taking her seat and closing the door. The road had very little traffic, it being late afternoon and too early for the office crowds to fill the roads. When they reached, she alighted and paid the taxi driver. She stepped on to the wide footpath towards the Maidan side and began walking along the pathway, crowded with balloon sellers, ice-cream carts, *chanachur wallahs* and *puchka wallahs*. She spotted Kunal striding towards her, a big smile on his face.

"You came," he remarked, as soon as he reached her.

"Why?" she asked, offended. "You think I'm too scared to

come out on my own?"

"You're learning fast," he replied, deftly steering her towards a *puchka wallah*, as golpuppas were called in Calcutta.

The puchka wallah handed them small cones made of dried *saal* leaves, and while they looked on, stuffed a crisp puchka with a mixture of mashed, boiled potatoes and yellow *matar* before dipping it in the vessel containing the spicy *"jeera and imli" pani*. The *puchkas* were delicious and Kunal had four of them, while she wanted two more.

Kunal paid and turned to go back the way he had come.

"You're leaving already?" she asked, disappointed. "I can't beleive this...you called me all the way from Alipore just to spend fifteen minutes with me."

She was walking fast, trying to keep up with him.

"My work is very important to me, Renee; I have a meeting in exactly ten minutes."

"That's not fair!" she protested, almost running to keep up with his long strides. "We could have taken a walk in the Maidan..."

He stopped for a moment, before crossing Chowringhee Road. "Meet me same time, same place next Monday and we'll spend more time together."

I'm not coming again for just a few puchkas, Renee thought, as she turned back to get a taxi and go home. What does Kunal think of himself, ordering me around like this? I may not come at all, she thought, as the taxi took a left turn towards Race Course Road.

She was there, though, the next Monday, wearing her pink churidar kurta and looked around for him the minute she got down from her taxi. This time, he was waiting for her, wearing dark grey trousers and a cream coloured shirt. He wasted no time in buying two chocolate ice cream bars from the Kwality cart close by, and beckoned her to follow him. He stopped near one of the numerous trees spread all over the Maidan, where a few people could be seen in animated conversation. It was a public place which provided space for private conversations in the teeming metroplolis of Calcutta. They found a mound of grass under a shady tree and sat down. Renee carefully unwrapped her "choco- bar" and bit into the crispy chocolate layer with vanilla ice cream beneath it.

He came straight to the point, "What are your future plans Renee?"

"I want to settle down, of course," she said. "I want my own home...many of my friends are engaged to be married..." she trailed off.

Kunal was watching her intently, as he ate his own ice cream.

"You're not interested in taking up a job for a year or two?" he asked. "You could gain valuable work experience," he suggested.

"No Kunal," she replied, shaking her head. She rose and paced about slowly. "I do not want to waste my time sitting in a drab office from nine to five. I want my own home. I want to go shopping, I want to go to parties..."

"...like all girls your age," he completed her sentence. He rose and joined her. "I have many responsibilities to fulfill," he continued thoughtfully. "First of all, I want to make sure I am financially secure before I can think of settling down. Secondly, I have to get my younger sister Ragini married first...she's the same age as you...just completed her graduation."

They began walking towards the many sports Clubs dotting the other end of the Maidan. Renee was confused. As she walked alongside Kunal, she could feel the strong pull, the sense of completeness she felt whenever she was with him. She liked talking to him and wanted to spend more time with him. She understood Kunal was asking her to wait for him, without directly expressing it in so many words. Renee was torn between her desire to have a deeper understanding and relationship with a strong and steadfast man like Kunal, and her wish to have an easy and comfortable life immediately. Renee did not wish to wait for an uncertain future; she knew there was going to be no commitment from either of them at this point of time.

Kunal looked at his watch, and turning around began walking fast towards the pavement.

"I have to rush back to office, Renee" he said. "Take a taxi and get back home safely."

She wanted to say something more but realized he was bringing their conversation to a close. "Bye Kunal," she said, and began to walk briskly, even as he did not look back, but continued walking to reach his office and catch up on his work. Deep within her heart Renee hoped she had made the right decision in letting Kunal go to lead his own life, even as she tried to move forward with her own.

CHAPTER 10

MARRIAGE

At the dinner table the next evening, Renee's father made a surprise announcement. He said that he was going to send a proposal to Mr. Rajeshwar Varma to discuss the possibility of Renee's marriage with his son Rajdeep. She was shocked at his sudden decision.

"*Papa!*" she cried, "What are you saying?"

"You heard right," he responded firmly, "Your mother and I have to settle your marriage. It is our responsibility. You said you do not wish to work or study any further." He was hungry and he stretched out his hand for the bowl of delicious chicken curry, and took a good helping. He broke off a corner of the hot chapatti and dipped it in the thick gravy.

"Yes Renee," her mother quickly interceded, "At your age, I was a married woman."

Renee was taken aback and at a loss for words. She stared from one parent to the other......she felt cornered.

"What's the hurry?" she protested. "I've only recently completed my graduation. I'm not that old *Mamoni*, that you should start worrying. Besides, times have changed."

Renee's father was getting exasperated. He replaced his spoon on his plate and turned towards his daughter, giving her an ultimatum. "Listen Renee," he said slowly, "Either you return to Lucknow, stay in the hostel and study for your M.A. or you let us go ahead with this proposal."

"You have met Rajdeep," her mother reminded her. "You seem to enjoy his company. He took you out to Trincas the other evening. What's your problem now? What will people say if we let you go out with boys like that?"

Renee was furious. What will people say? Is that all that mattered to her parents? For her, it was the question of her whole life. She had no appetite for the tasty kheer served for dessert after dinner. She ate a few spoons, and pushed the bowl aside.

She rose from the table and said, "Please give me time to think things over. I'll let you know my decision soon. Good night."

She rushed to her bedroom and sank on the bed. She was confused; she did not know what she wanted to do. She dozed off to sleep and her mother came later and quietly switched off the light.

Renee woke next morning, after a restful night's sleep, and sat up in bed, trying to think clearly. Of one thing she was absolutely certain: she did not wish to study any further. She had worked hard in school and college and got good grades. What was the purpose of completing her M.A. if she was not going to work? She would have to return to the hostel and go through the drudgery of reading Chaucer and Milton and study linguistics and the history of English Literature. She wanted to get married and set up her own home and live a life of comfort. She was fully aware that her father would retire in a few years, and though there had been enough for all their daily needs, the family was used to managing on a tight budget. Her younger brothers would soon be completing their studies, and would require their father's support in settling in life. At the breakfast table, she told her parents to go ahead and send a proposal to Rajdeep's parents. She liked Rajdeep and enjoyed his company. Besides, he was always kind and courteous to her. At her age and with her limited experience, this seemed sufficient grounds for Renee to believe that she and Rajdeep could build a future together.

Mr. Srivastava sent a formal proposal, along with her recent photograph, to the Varmas. They accepted the proposal and soon Renee and Rajdeep got engaged. *Bauji*, Ma, Rajdeep and other family members came to their house with gifts and mithai. There was a formal ring exchanging ceremony. Her brothers were thrilled that their *Didi* was going to get married.

One Sunday evening, a few days after their engagement, Rajdeep had parked his car near the entrance of Lakeview Club. Renee was walking up to join him, wearing a peacock blue sari, a pearl string around her slim neck, and high heels. She had left her hair open and it framed her pretty face. She was glowing. Kunal had come to the Club for a while, having nothing better to do in his flat. He was returning home, when he saw her walking towards Rajdeep's car, who was sitting in the driver's seat, waiting for her to join him.

As he approached Renee, he stopped and addressed her, "Are going out somewhere?"

She had stopped to settle the folds of her sari. When she

looked up, she met his gaze directly. "I'm getting married to Rajdeep," she said softly.

"Oh! Congratulations!" he said, surprised by her annoncement. He continued in his warm voice, "I wish the two of you happiness together."

Renee thanked him and went to join her fiance.

Kunal hoped she had made the right choice and not agreed under pressure from her parents. There is no point in thinking of her now, he told himself. Very soon she is going to be another man's wife and start a new life. The loud honking of a car interrupted his reverie, and he hastily stepped aside to make way for Rajdeep's car as he drove off, with Renee on the seat beside to him.

Mr. Srivastava visited the Varmas for the first time and was duly impressed by their beautiful and well kept house. He was pleased his daughter would be going into a family where she could live a life of comfort and luxury. He could see they were well off and Rajdeep also had a good job. His daughter would never have to worry about money and to him it mattered a lot. Her future mother-in-law seemed a pleasant person; he fervently hoped his headstrong daughter would be able to get along with her, as they would be staying together in the same house. After refreshments and tea had been served, Mr. Varma wanted to discuss details of the wedding: how many people to bring for the baraat, the gifts to be exchanged, what the bride's family was giving as her trousseau. It was decided the baraat would come to Lakeview Club and the mandap for the marriage ceremony was to be erected in the front lawns.

When father returned after finalizing the details, *Mamoni*

went into a tizzy. Lists had to be made for buying clothes and other necessary items for Renee's wedding. Mother and daughter went shopping for saris to Gariahat Market, they dashed off to New Market for handbags and foot wear. Her parents took her to the best jewellery stores, to choose what she wanted to buy. They gave her a beautiful and generous trousseau and in her heart Renee would always be grateful for that. For their son-in-law, they ordered a suit to his size and a gold ring. In addition, her father gave him a check to buy anything the young couple would require as they began their new journey in life.

Renee's father contacted a pandit, and an auspicious date and time were selected for the occasion, towards the end of November. They spent considerable time choosing the wedding card from the samples father brought home. Once it was selected, he placed the order for the number of cards he wanted printed. Names and addresses of relatives and friends were tabulated, and written out on the envelopes. Once the postage stamps had been pasted, he took them with him to office and dropped them at the nearest Post box.

Relatives started arriving two days before the wedding; arrangements had been made to put them up in various guest houses. *Mamoni* had stocked her store room with grocery, spices and every other possible ingredient required for Indian cooking. In addition, a professional cook, along with two assistants, had been hired for those days. Umer Singh and their ayah worked overtime to give their "Baby Renee" a grand wedding. Jatin and Sonu arrived from College, and dashed off to the market to buy new clothes and be measured for their first suits.

On the evening of the wedding, the Club was lit up with

multi-colored lights, and a mandap had been put up on the front lawns. The pandit arrived exactly at five and sat inside making preparations. Dinner was going to be served to the baraatis on one side of the lawn and the waiters were busy, laying out various items on the tables. The baraat arrived on time, to a shimmer of bright lights from large, portable lamps, held aloft by six men wearing red and gold uniforms. A costumed band followed on foot playing the song,

Bharaon phool barsaon

Mera Mehboob ayaa hain...."

Renee looked beautiful as a bride, dressed in a red and gold Benarasi silk sari, wearing her heaviest gold jewellery. *Mamoni* had insisted she cover her head with the sari pallu and she sat demurely with lowered eyes on the sofa inside the Club hall. Rajdeep looked dashing in a gold embroidered sherwani and churidar pyjamas. As he walked ahead, his family members and close friends followed him, the younger ones breaking into an impromptu dance to the beat of the catchy tune. The women were resplendent in Banarasi brocade and Kanjeevaram silk saris, laden with heavy jewellery. The men mostly wore suits, it being winter. After the jaimaal, the guests were served mithai and various kinds of sherbet, while the bride and groom walked to the mandap for the wedding ceremony. Once they were seated, the pandit asked for Renee's father and mother to sit on a small durrie behind her and similarly, Rrajdeep's parents sat beside him.

Once the wedding was over, the happy couple went around touching their elders' feet to seek their blessings for their new life ahead. A sumptuous meal had been laid out in the meantime, and the guests made their way to the tempting array of dishes spread out on the long dining tables on one side of the lawn. There was a small lunch at Renee's house the next day for only close relatives. Rajdeep had gone home the previous night after the wedding, and came the next morning to fetch his bride and take her home. A few young cousins accompanied him and they sat with their shy, new Bhabhi in the drawing room engaging her in talk and jokes, trying to get to know her better. A vegetarian meal was served and everyone enjoyed the home cooked food.

As the time for leaving her home approached, Renee felt a lump in her throat. Her new suitcases and other luggage were brought out, to be loaded on to the two cars parked near the front porch. Renee wept as she bid farewell to her parents and two brothers, and clung to *Mamoni* in tears. Her mother said goodbye to the intelligent, self-willed daughter she loved so much, and hoped she would be able to find a place for herself in her new home. Rajdeep gently escorted his new wife to the car, in which the others were already sitting. As the car began moving Mamoni waved to her beloved daughter, and wiping her tears, went back into her own home.

Chapter 11

New Beginnings And Motherhood

In her new home Renee met Ashok, Pallavi and their daughter Sonia, who had come to attend the wedding, and was able to spend time with them and get to know them better. Rajdeep's sister Pinky and her husband had come from Dhanbad and returned after spending another week in Calcutta. Renee did her best to adjust to her new life with the Varma family. She enjoyed dressing up and going out during the weekends with Rajdeep and his friends, some of whom had only recently got married. Since the household was run by Mrs. Varma, she had no role to play in its daily supervision. She passed her time by reading books or going for a walk in the garden and began taking an interest in the flowers and vegetables being grown there. The mali, eager to please the new bahurani, followed any instructions she cared to give. In spite of these activities, Renee began to feel lonely during the day: she missed the company of her College friends and the light hearted banter with *Mamoni*. She remembered wistfully how she would badger her mother with silly questions and pull her leg over small things and at the end of it all, they would laugh together. Most of all, she missed the independence she had been used to, to do as she pleased and speak up her mind openly. Her parents had always included her in any discussion, and given due weightage to her opinions. In her new home, it was almost like being a voiceless person. She was expected to be silent when others spoke, and express her views only to her husband and that too, in the privacy of her bedroom.

Other problems arose: one was regarding Renee's covering her head with the sari pallu. She noticed that when Ashok bhaiya and his wife visited them, Pallavi roamed around the house with her head uncovered. She wore sleeveless blouses for parties at their friend's homes, or when all of them went out together for meals at restaurants. *Bauji* and Ma never objected to anything she did. They were well aware that their elder son would not tolerate any comments about his wife. On the other hand, Renee was expected to cover her head with the sari whenever she was in the presence of *Bauji*. He himself did not say anything, and perhaps would not have minded or even noticed if she did not do so, but this rule was imposed by her mother-in-law. Even though Renee found it increasingly inconvenient to do so, she did her best to wrap it tightly around her head. She tried pointing out to Rajdeep that there were too many curbs on her freedom; either he did not hear or pretended not to hear. Renee began to feel it was unfair of her in-laws to impose rules on her. The more she showed her resentment, the more Ma was insistent on Renee's falling in line. She had made many sacrifices for her sons' welfare and proper education; she was going to make sure at least the younger daughter-in-law did as she was told to do.

There was conflict also between Sheila Varma and Renee over the latter's duties in the kitchen. Mrs.Varma spent her mornings in the kitchen, preparing treats for her family, with the help of Bansi. Snacks like nimkis, besan ladoos, fried chirwa and peanuts were made and stored in clean, air tight jars. Her family enjoyed them with their evening tea or in between meals. Pickles were prepared in the mango season during the hot, summer months. Renee watched with keen interest as the freshest raw mangoes were bought from the market, washed and cut into small pieces, placed in an open cane basket and left out in the sun to dry. The next step was to add all the necessary spices, turmeric, salt and mustard oil and mix these thoroughly. Finally, it was all stored in clean porcelain jars and set aside to mature. No doubt it tasted delicious but Renee considered it a waste of her time and education. She had absolutely no interest in pickle making. Ma even made lemonade at home when lemons were in season, and cheap. Naturally, she expected her daughter-in-law to assist her strenuous efforts rather than sit comfortably reading books. Renee had a simple solution for this: go to the market and buy a bottle of pickle and lemonade. Call it stubbornness, but she refused to be bullied into doing anything she did not believe in.

Rajdeep was clear about his views: if his mother was going to enter the kitchen, it was Renee's duty to follow her and offer assistance. Renee began to feel let down by her husband. She had expected support from him to live a life of fulfilment where she could develop her own potential. Instead she was expected to bow to his family's every wish, no matter how unreasonable. Most of the time, though, Rajdeep paid her the attention Renee craved for; she had made friends with some of his colleagues' wives and enjoyed going out in groups with them. These were fun times spent in their company but they were restricted to holidays or weekends.

Renee was overjoyed to discover she was going to become a mother. When Rajdeep heard the news he gave her a tight hug and could not stop smiling. When she held her son Abhishek in her arms for the first time, Renee gazed at him in awe and wonder, even as he felt hungry and let out a gutsy cry that sent his parents into a tizzy. The nurse came in, to teach Renee how to nurse the baby. Holding him she felt complete in a way she had never felt before. *Bauji* and Ma came to the hospital to see him and and he sent them into swoons of delight by deciding to smile at them. Once back home with Abhishek, they settled into their bedroom on the first floor of the house. Days flew by in a whirl of nappy changes, baby's yells for food, and his sound and restful sleep. Rajdeep proved to be a surprisingly hands on father, and could soon deftly change a nappy.

When Abhishek was three months old, Renee started bringing him downstairs to spend the day in the pram in the back verandah. He gurgled and made cute baby sounds and each time his doting grandparents responded with delighted surprise and discussed excitedly how sweet their grandson was. When Rajdeep's sister, Pinky, came to visit them from Dhanbad, she came laden with gifts for her nephew. She was thrilled to become an aunt and showered him with love and spent time playing with him when he came downstairs with his mother.

While life went on pleasantly for Rajdeep and Renee, things were beginning to get difficult for the senior Mr. Varma. He was getting on in years, and his Liluah factory was no longer doing as well as before. The Ambassador cars were facing fierce competition from newer and cheaper models introduced in the market. With customers clamouring for the lighter and sleeker models flooding the market, the orders for the sturdy Ambassador cars, being manufactured by Hindustan Motors, were greatly reduced, in spite of the fact that it was the preferred vehicle in use by government departments. This directly impacted the auto ancillary suppliers and the factory at Liluah was no longer working at optimum capacity. With both his sons branching out on their own, Mr. Varma increasingly felt unable to shoulder the burden of running the factory alone. Mrs. Varma, too, was finding it difficult to maintain and run such a large household with advancing years and a tighter budget. She began voicing her problems to her son, Rajdeep, to get his sympathy and support. He would express his concern, and assure her that things were bound to improve. Yet, his parents began to feel that Rajdeep was showering too much attention on his family. It was strange that while Sheila Varma could be such an affectionate and caring grandmother to Abhishek, she should make his mother the butt of her frustrations. As the household budget got reduced, she began to harbor resentment for her daughter- in -law's "luxurious" lifestyle, although the family problems were none of her fault.

When Abhishek was about two years old, Renee was thrilled to discover that she was pregnant again. The second pregnancy was hard on her; she was left to take care of Abhishek on her own with the help of the maid. Her days were busy, taking care of a toddler, in addition to the rest her Doctor had asked her to take. She craved for attention from Rajdeep, but he no longer seemed to have the time to fuss over her, and make her feel precious, as only a loving husband can do. On the other hand, his mother's behavior towards her worsened; she began complaining to her son about his wife's expenses and her independent views. Rajdeep tried his best to ignore her complaints and never mentioned anything about it to Renee.

After many years of service in the railways, Renee's father retired and decided to settle down in Lucknow, where some of his old friends and relatives lived. Renee's parents were familiar with the city, having lived there earlier, and rented a flat in the residential locality of Mahanagar, where they set up house after they left Calcutta. Renee missed them a lot; her visits to Lakeview Park had provided her with a safety outlet, where she could vent her emotions and relax for a few hours. She had loved walking up to Alipore Park Road with Abhishek in her arms and taking a taxi to her parents house. His grandparents doted on him and he wandered all over the house, happily exploring the new surroundings. Renee enjoyed having her favourite coffee, made just way she liked it, and unwinding with her mother. *Mamoni* heard her out patiently, but cautioned her to behave herself with her in-laws. Her father warned her never to cross boundaries. Renee did not know what to make of their advice: it may have worked for them, but she belonged to another generation and was not very sure if it was at all applicable in the changing times. What she cherished was the love and pampering she received for a few hours, until it was time for her and Abhishek to go home.

Her growing up years in the railway colonies had given Renee precious memories which she would always cherish. Mr.Srivastava was allowed to keep the house one month after his retirement while he made arrangements to relocate to Lucknow. The day finally arrived when packing of their furniture started and within three days it was all done and ready to be loaded on to a truck. Rajdeep had taken time out from work to help with the loading and bid farewell to his in-laws. Renee waved a tearful goodbye to her parents as they drove off to the station. She knew too, that she was bidding farewell to a carefree and sheltered phase of her life, and from now onwards she would have to manage things entirely on her own.

Renee noticed a subtle change in her in-laws attitude after her father's retirement. In small ways, they reminded her of her place in the household as a daughter-in-law, as if what she had to say, no longer mattered. They were less mindful of her needs. By the time her second son Gaurav was born, their attitude had changed completely. While she craved for loving attention, she was met with cool indifference. They were aware that she was financially dependent on Rajdeep; she had to behave herself, for her own sake, and for those of her sons. For the first time Renee regretted not having studied for her M.A. She had scored brilliantly in her B.A. examinations and her father had been keen she should study further or sit for the competitive exams. How foolish and vain she had been! She had thought she could have a life of comfort and luxury without working for it. Renee was learning fast that life was not so simple, and that reality could be harsh.

The factory began making losses due to reduced demand for auto parts by Hindustan Motors. Consequently staff salary had to be reduced, and there was less money *Bauji* brought home. Much against his wishes, he had to lay off two shop floor workers. He asked Ma to tighten up the household budget. The first thing she did was sack Abhishek and Gaurav's full time ayah. That left Renee to take care of an energetic three and a half year old, as well as a baby who had just begun crawling all over the place. She had to use all her ingenuity to take care of them, as well as make time for herself for leisure and adequate rest. On the other hand, Mrs. Verma's writ ran in the house; even on a tight budget, she went about her daily household activities as before. She learnt to cut wasteful expenditure and made good use of left over food to dish out appetizing dishes for her family; she proved to be a skillful manager as well.

Rajdeep was doing well in his career; he was given a promotion and was spending more time now at work than before. Even though she felt happy for her husband, Renee began to feel neglected at home. Her days went by in a whirl of caring for her boys, and the outings with Rajdeep became few and far between. She met very few people her age and craved for company. On the other hand, Rajdeep spent his day with his colleagues, engaged in meaningful work, and his confidence grew by leaps and bounds.

Renee was aware that life had changed drastically for her parents: gone were the days of big bungalows with lush, green lawns and servants quarters. Renee and her sons had visited them in their rented flat in Lucknow, and been lavished with love and affection. There were special treats waiting for them. *Mamoni* had ordered the part time cook to make her favourite chicken curry and pulao for dinner the day they reached. It was good to be home. Abhishek got busy playing with his doting grandfather and Gaurav ran around exploring all corners. She saw the changes in her parent's lifestyle and was amazed at how well they had adjusted. She said nothing to them of her own troubles; she let them believe she led a happy life in Calcutta. Yet her parents were quick to notice that their vivacious daughter was quiter than before, and hesitated to express her views freely. She had become reticent and accepted whatever was given to her gratefully. Worse, they noticed her loss of confidence and hoped it was only a passing phase and things would improve with time for their beloved Renee.

In their home in Calcutta, *Bauji* and Ma lavished their love and care on their grandsons. For Renee, however, life had changed in ways she had not imagined possible. For her, the house in Alipore Park Road was like a prison. She found the restrictions stifling: she longed for the days of cycle rides, sitting pillion behind Sacchu, with the cool wind blowing against her hair. Renee had completely stopped going out on her own. She insisted that she be allowed some independence; after much thought, Rajdeep agreed to let her take a cab to New Market. The highlight of her day was going to fetch Abhishek from the Primary School where he studied, in nearby New Road. Rajdeep would drop him to school in his car, on his way to office in the morning. She would walk down to fetch him around one in the afternoon, leaving Gaurav in the care of his grandmother. She loved getting out of the house and enjoyed the sense of freedom it gave her just to be able to walk to the nearby school. She waited outside it's gates, along with the other mothers, *dadus*, drivers and maids. The dispersal bell rang loudly, and the children would come running out, pushing each other, laughing and shouting for joy to go home. Her son would hold her hand trustingly, as they began their short walk home.

The life she now lead, was bound to take it's toll on Renee's confidence. Even though she had been allowed to stop covering her head with the sari pallu, she found no joy in this small achievement. Her days were restricted to the boundaries of a home and she had very little contact with the jostling, thriving world outside; she was very lonely. Somewhere along the way she had lost the spring in her step and her infectious laughter. When Rajdeep returned from work in the evenings, he expected her to dress up and greet him with a smile. She could not do so, because she would have had a long day with the kids, and felt tired and worn out. She herself needed love and support.

"Can't you smile Renee, for a change?" he asked her one evening, "....when you hand me my tea?"

She sighed. "I've had a long day, Rajdeep," she replied. "The children have been very naughty. Gaurav broke a flower vase in the drawing room and I had to clear up the mess and pick up the shards of glass pieces from the floor. In the afternoon, Ma insisted I help her in making nimkis."

"So it's always someone else's fault! You are never to blame," he snapped.

Renee was shocked at the virulence in his voice.

"I mean..." she began feebly, "I get tired too..."

"And I have a cushy job, is that it?" he interrupted her, in a raised voice.

"Don't shout," she requested him, her voice low. "Others will hear."

He was in no mood to listen to her. "What of that?" he retorted sharply.

Renee was deeply hurt by Rajdeep's behaviour. In her growing sense of isolation from the rest of the family, she had believed she could depend on her husband for support, but now she doubted even that. She sighed... how much he had changed from when she had first met him at Lakeview Club He knew he could not abandon his parents after Ashok bhaiya had made a decision to lead an independent life with his family. Whatever it was, Rajdeep had no business to hurt her feelings like this.

He rose with his tea cup in hand, and strode angrily towards the door.

Renee got up and ran after him, "I'm sorry if I was rude. Please sit with me!"

Her entreaty fell on deaf ears; he was out of the door and running lightly down the steps, balancing his cup in one hand. He went and joined his parents, who were having their own tea, in the back verandah. After dinner that evening, back in their bedroom, Rajdeep neither said sorry nor tried to make up in any way. She longed for someone to hold her close and make her feel safe.

Next morning, after Rajdeep left for work, and Abhishek and Gaurav, who had recently joined nursery, were in school, Renee went for a walk in the garden; no matter what problems she was facing, she never lost hope. She remembered *Mamoni's* unconditional love, and her father's firm guidance. She recalled the many obstacles Anita, Sacchu and she had overcome to find *Dadaji's* gift. She knew in her heart that she was going to find a way out of her current situation.

BOOK TWO

CHAPTER 12

LEAVING HOME

It was the year 1982, and Renee and Rajdeep had been married for ten years. Abhishek was nine years old and studying in class four and Gaurav was six and in class one. They went to a prestigious boys school in a car pool along with three other children from Alipore Park Road.

Renee and Rajdeep had been having problems in their marriage since the last few years. It centred around her desire to be independent as a person, along with her need to feel a sense of emotional security. She herself failed to understand why, even after having spent so many years with the Varmas, she did not feel a part of the family. Her sons were happily growing up in the household, and enjoyed the visits of their various uncles, aunts and cousins. Much as Renee wanted to, there was a part of her, which could not open up to anyone. Renee began to wonder if it had anything to do with her childhood trauma of having been abandoned as a child of three and a half, along with her younger brother Jatin, who was ten months old at that time, when their parents left them and went to the United States of America in the year 1954. Her father had accepted a year's scholarship with Harvard University, under a scheme sponsored by President Dwight D. Eisenhower to give grants to young married couples from all over the world, to come to the Harvard campus and do a management course for a year. They were given accommodation in the married quarters, and the idea behind the scheme was to promote fellowship among people of different countries. Renee's father was offered the scholarship and decided to accept it, and take *Mamoni* along, leaving their two young children behind in India. Renee and Jatin were left in the care of their ayah in their uncle's home and stayed with his family. Renee began to wonder if the insecurity she felt, had any connection with the separation from her mother for almost a year and a half as a small child.

Renee had such deep insecurities that perhaps no husband would have been able to provide the emotional support she needed. She knew Rajdeep tried his best, but there were many others in the family she had to deal with and not all of them were kind to her. Mrs. Sheila Varma had been wary of Renee from the time she first met her; she found the girl too outspoken for her liking, and too westernized in her ways. Rajdeep seemed charmed by his wife and catered to all her demands. Mrs.Varma was well aware she would have to depend on her younger son to take care of her and her husband in their old age and help her consolidate their property. She felt she was sole mistress of her domain and guarded her position fiercely. She had wanted a docile daughter-in-law who would be obedient, but it seemed Renee challenged her position at every step.

Their clash over the dinner menu was waiting to happen. It was a Wednesday afternoon, and Renee had gone to New Market for shopping. She had bought all she needed and stopped at Nahoum's bakery where the air was filled with the delicious aroma of freshly baked goods displayed at the counters: fruit cakes, pastries, tarts, macaroons, cheese straws, special brownies, bread sticks and a variety of buns and breads. She bought a fruit cake and then moving to the grocery shop next to it, bought a packet of noodles, a small bottle of soya sauce and vinegar. She remembered the delicious Chowmien Umer Singh made at home and wanted to cook it for her sons. She made her way to the huge vegetable section and bought carrots, beans, spring onions and two pieces of green peppers.

Renee returned home to find the boys playing football in the back lawn. She went upstairs to her bedroom and deposited the shopping bags and her purse on the table. She looked at her watch: four o'clock already. She decided to cook the Chowmein and have it ready for the children's dinner which they ate every evening by seven pm. When she entered the kitchen she found it deserted: Bansi had retired for his afternoon break after cleaning the kitchen counter and washing all the utensils which had been left on the countertop to dry. Although she had never liked cooking she found she enjoyed making dishes which Rajdeep and her sons relished. She put the noodles to boil in a large *dekchi*, washed and thinly sliced the vegetables she had bought, on a wooden chopping board. The green peppers she cut in two halves, removed the seeds, washed and finely sliced these too.

In a *kadai* she heated some cooking oil, sauted the diced spring onions and added the carrots, beans and green peppers. She stir fried for a minute, then measured out and added some soya sauce, vinegar and a little tomato ketchup. A delicious aroma filled the kitchen. While she was straining the boiled noodles she heard the kitchen door being yanked open. It was her mother-in-law.

"Renee!" she cried, sounding agitated, "What are you doing here?"

"Making noodles for the children's dinner Ma. They love to eat Chowmein when we go to restaurants," replied Renee, continuing to stir the vegetables in the *kadai*.

"Eat it when you go out," rejoined Mrs. Varma sternly, "Don't cook it in my kitchen. Why didn't you take my permission before deciding to make it?"

"Take your permission?" asked Renee incredulously. The noodles were done; she switched off the gas, strained them in a soup strainer and put the lot in a bowl, which she covered with a lid. She turned towards her mother-in-law, "You mean I need your permission to cook here?"

"Yes, you do," said Mrs. Varma, stamping her right foot and putting her hands on her hips. She continued to stare at Renee menacingly. "Don't forget this is my house and my kitchen."

Renee tossed her head, "I live here now and I can do as I please," she said defiantly.

Mrs. Varma said nothing but left the kitchen and went straight upstairs to her bedroom. Renee felt so small. She began to regret having decided to buy the noodles in the first place. Her only happiness came when Abhishek and Gaurav sat for dinner that evening and loved the chowmein she had cooked for them.

"It's delicious Mummy! Can I have some more?" Abhishek asked stretching out his plate.

"Of course!" replied his mother, serving him a large helping.

Not to be outdone by his elder brother, Gaurav stuffed his mouth with a large spoonful and held up his hand, "I want too," he mumbled with his mouth full of food.

"Gaurav!" his mother admonished him, "Finish your food first. There's plenty more." He nodded happily when she piled on more of the noodles and vegetables on his plate. Dinner over, the boys went to their room upstairs to wash up and went to bed. They had school the next morning.

Bauji and Rajdeep returned from work and relaxed with their cups of tea and a light snack. Ma refused to come downstairs to join them; she said she had a headache. Rajdeep went upstairs to check on her and was closeted with his mother for nearly half an hour. When he returned, he was livid with Renee for having been rude to his mother.

"I never said anything to her," she replied, laying out four dinner plates on the dining table.

"You have upset Ma," he accused his wife "Where was the need to cook all this stuff?" His harsh tone hurt Renee because she had expected him to see things from her point of view; instead, he was making unjust accusations. She had not had the intention of insulting her mother-in-law: all she wanted was the freedom to do as she wished. Too many people in this house seem to have problems with my living here, thought Renee. It was only a fleeting thought, and she let it pass.

She turned towards her husband and tried to reason with him, "You know very well how much the boys love to eat this when we go out."

"Exactly my point," he said. She noticed his sharp tone. "You should have kept it for outings, Renee. And not cooked it in my mother's kitchen."

"In your mother's kitchen, Rajdeep?" Renee inquired in a hurt voice, but he wasn't listening and had walked out of the room.

Bauji entered, took his seat and served himself the aloo matar curry. He had no idea of the row between his wife and daughter-in-law. Rajdeep joined his father at the dining table, and ate in silence. However, Mrs. Varma refused to join them. After he had finished eating, Rajdeep washed his hands and serving two parathas and some vegetables on a plate, took it up to his mother's room. Renee sat with *Bauji*, while he finished his meal.

"Did you make this chowmein?" he asked her.

"Yes I did," she replied, "Abhishek and Gaurav like it a lot."

"It's well made," commented *Bauji*. "One last spoon," he said helping himself to a serving.

Renee was touched by the way *Bauji* went out of his way to make her feel comfortable and appreciated any little thing she did for him.

"Thank you, *Bauji*," she said, grateful that he had praised her cooking.

When he had finished his dinner he rose, and slowly walked up the stairs to go to his room. Renee stood forlorn on the landing, holding on to the bannister for some kind of support. She felt a tightness in her chest. She stood there, waiting for Rajdeep to come downstairs, her sense of rejection complete. Try as she might, she could not understand the change in his attitude towards her. Whatever the reason for his behavior, she felt trapped and upset. It added to her sense of insecurity. In a while he came downstairs, ignored her completely, and handed the empty plate to Bansi, who was clearing up the left overs. Renee and Rajdeep went up to their bedroom together but did not speak to each other. She lay on her side of the bed and cried herself to sleep that night.

The next day Rajdeep made up with Renee, in his own way. They were talking again, and best of all, enjoying each other's company. That weekend they took the children to the Alipore zoo and everyone had fun. It was winter and very pleasant outdoors. It was announced that one of *Bauji's* old friends would be coming for dinner the next Sunday. The elderly couple would be accompanied by their son and daughter-in-law, who stayed with them in their Ballygunge house. Renee dressed with care in a printed, pink and navy blue silk sari. She wore a matching embroidered blouse with Gurjari mirror work on the sleeves. She left her hair open, pinned lightly at the sides to keep it neat. She wore the exact same shade of pink lipstick, put kajal in the eyes and a small maroon bindi on her forehead. She looked pretty and went to the drawing room feeling happy and at peace.

The guests arrived around eight in the evening, and were warmly received by *Bauji* and Ma, and ushered into their large drawing room. Abhishek and Gaurav had eaten their dinner earlier and gone up to bed. Rajdeep and Renee were introduced to the family and they sat together in one corner near the radiogram, while the elders sat on the sofas near the centre. *Bauji* had much to catch up with his friend of many years. Drinks and snacks were shown around and the sound of animated talk filled the room. Soon dinner was announced, and everyone made their way into the dining room. A vast array of sumptuous dishes had been laid out on the table. Ma had been working with Bansi in the kitchen since the afternoon and the chicken biryani and dahi bara she had made looked delicious. Birju ran in and out of the kitchen bringing hot palak puris and all the guests relished the food served to them. Dinner over, the guests sat in the drawing room where kheer, topped with almonds and raisins, was served in small glass bowls. Soon it was time for the guests to leave. After seeing them off to their cars, *Bauji* and Rajdeep went upstairs. It was already past eleven and they had to leave for work early next morning.

Renee was feeling thirsty, and went to the kitchen to drink a glass of water.

"Renee!" she heard her mother-in-law call out sharply to her from the drawing room. She was surprised to hear her mother-in-law's voice: it meant she had not gone upstairs with the others. When she entered the drawing room she found Ma sitting on the large sofa near the coffee table, on which lay the empty dessert bowls.

"Pick these up, and take them to the kitchen sink," she said shortly, pointing to the used dishes.

Renee was taken aback at this sudden command.

"Why?" she inquired. She wanted to go upstairs and sleep; the party had been such a wonderful change for her and she wanted to put away her beautiful sari in her cupboard and wear her nighty and wash her make up. "Where's Birju?"

Mrs. Varma replied, sounding casual, "I told him to have his dinner."

"He always clears up after parties," Renee reminded her. "It's part of his job."

"He was very tired, so I gave him time off, and told him he could carry his food to his room and report for work tomorrow morning."

"Alright. So he'll clean this up tomorrow," said Renee, turning to go out of the door.

"No!" retorted Mrs. Varma sharply, her voice edgy, "You clean it up just now. Get a tray from the kitchen, and carry these back and put them near the sink."

Renee stopped and stared at her. Ma was doing this intentionally to show her that she could order her around and get her to do exactly as she pleased, no matter how smart and beautiful she thought she was. Even though Renee was filled with resentment, she swallowed her pride and picked up the dirty dishes and took them to the kitchen. When all of them had been removed, Mrs. Varma rose imperiuosly and went upstairs to her room.

Renee was upset and angry by the time she entered her bedroom. Rajdeep was sitting up in bed, reading a thriller by James Hadley Chase. She entered in a hurry, her face taut with supressed rage, banging the door shut behind her.

"Softly!" he cried, "You'll wake up the others."

"I can't live like this any longer !" cried Renee, her voice shaking.

"Why?, What's the matter?" he looked up surprised, putting

away his book. He gestured with his hands for her to come and sit beside him on the bed.

"Tell me, what has happened tonight to upset you so much?" he asked.

She sat beside him and told him in detail about what had happened downstairs after the party was over, and everyone had left. He heard her out patiently and remarked, "It's a small matter Renee. Don't over-react. Perhaps Ma wanted the used bowls removed before she retired for the night."

"It's not a question of cleaning up, Rajdeep!" exclaimed Renee. "I would have done it willingly myself. In any case, I do all my own work nowadays, ever since we sacked the ayah. It's the way your mother insists on humiliating me, and orders me around. I've taken it as long as I could. Not anymore."

Rajdeep was quiet for a while, as if thinking things out. "Be sensible Renee," he finally said, "and adjust to Ma's ways. Don't take everything she says to heart. Go and change and let's sleep. It's late."

Renee did not say anything, rising to fetch her nightdress. She went into the bathroom to change. When she returned, Rajdeep was fast asleep. She switched off the light, and lay on her side of the bed. The party she had looked forward to so much, had been ruined by her mother-in-law's willful and domineering behavior. She lay on the bed, wide awake. Sleep eluded her. It was the first time in her life she had lain awake all night. How she wished *Mamoni* was with her; she would have caressed her forehead lovingly and Renee would have instantly fallen asleep.

After tossing restlessly for most of the night, Renee slept and awoke at five in the morning. She brushed her teeth, and decided to make herself a cup of tea. In the kitchen, she found her mother-in-law pouring hot water into a tea pot.

"Up so early?" asked Mrs. Varma.

"Yes," replied Renee briefly.

"Don't show your temper to me so early in the morning," warned Mrs. Varma, adding sugar to her tea. "You should learn to adjust to those elder to you in this family."

Renee did not reply, her head throbbing with tension.

"Learn what you are told to do, Renee," continued Mrs. Varma sharply, "Your father has retired from service. Your parents can no longer give you any support, financial or otherwise. Forget about your cushy life in your Railway Colony." She took her cup of tea, and walked triumphantly out of the kitchen. She had shown the girl her rightful place in the household.

Renee made herself a cup of tea and went to the back verandah, and sat on a stool near the edge of the lawn. Dawn was breaking and the trees were bathed in a golden light, the birds were beginning to chirp and a squirrel ran up the steps and looked inquiringly at her. Renee's mind was made up. She was going to work for a better life, and for her own happiness, from today.

She realized this was not how things were meant to be in her life. She remembered Sports Day in school, and saw herself marching proudly with the gently fluttering flag at the head of Blue team; her best friend Sara, so confident and full of self-belief, leading the Green team ahead of her. Where was

Sara now ? Renee was sure she was struggling for her share of happiness, even fighting for it, for the world was not going to yield, until one gave it a push. It is our birth right, thought Renee, what we were born to achieve. It was an immense struggle at times, but the important thing was to keep going and have faith in one self. She was ordering, in a loud, clear voice, "Baayein dekh" and marching Left right, Left right, as the girls following her, turned their heads sharply to the left. Seeing from the corner of her eyes, as she looked straight ahead, that *Mamoni* was smiling at her, she had felt unbeatable and ready to triumph over any challenge she would have to face in her life.

That morning, Renee made up her mind. It was not an easy decision to make, but the only way to rebuild her future. She decided to walk out of this big, beautiful house and work towards a life of self-respect and dignity. She had no idea where she would go; she would trust destiny to show her the way. She felt no fear as she walked out of the house the next afternoon. She kept some clothes in an overnight bag, picked up her handbag and stepped out of the gate. Rajdeep was in office, the boys in school, and *Bauji* and Ma were having their afternoon nap. Renee hailed a taxi and asked the driver to take her to Lindsay Street. She alighted at the Chowringhee Road T junction, and paid the taxi driver. She clutched her two bags and began walking towards Globe cinema. She had no idea why she had chosen to come here: perhaps, because she had been here earlier on countless occasions with her parents and brothers on family outings. Today she was alone; blinking back her tears, trying her best not to cry, she walked past the familiar shops with hurried steps. If only Sacchu were here, she thought longingly, he would have supported her and helped her find her way forward.

CHAPTER 13

SACCHU

When Sachhu saw Renee walking hurriedly on the Lindsay Street footpath, carrying a bag and her purse, he recognized her instantly, even though he had not met her since she had left Varanasi. She was dressed in a green churidar kurta, a chiffon dupatta covering her shoulders. He was sitting in Bata Shoe Shop, trying out black formal shoes. He dropped the shoe he had been trying out for size, pushed aside the amazed salesman, jumped over a stool and rushed barefoot out of the store. Renee was walking on the footpath teary eyed and feeling upset, not even sure where she was going: she ducked under handbags strung up for sale, past a large table displaying cheap sunglasses, men's leather belts and purses. She had crossed Globe cinema, when she felt someone tap her right shoulder. She spun around angrily to see who had dared to touch her and saw a barefoot young man, dressed in cream colored T shirt and blue jeans, smiling at her. When his mop of unruly hair fell on his forehead and he pushed it aside irritably, she knew it was Sacchu. He had grown so tall, and so handsome. Hastily she wiped her tears with her dupatta, but he could see she had been crying.

The gutsy girl who had been his classmate in school, and with whom he had shared so many adventures in the Manduadih Railway Colony, had grown up to be an attractive woman. What he did not like was her wan and dispirited look. He presumed she must be married by now, with a family of her own; he was also aware girls had a tough time adjusting to a new family after marriage, and had to make many compromises. His elder sister Anita, had been married to a businessman in Calcutta a few years earlier. There had been adjustment issues, of course, but no major problems as far as he could tell. Whatever had happened with Renee, she seemed unhappy.

"Sacchu!" she cried, "Whatever are you doing in Lindsay Street?"

"Exactly what you are doing," he replied, grinning, "Shopping!"

"And why are you shopping barefoot, of all things?" she asked, staring at his feet.

He threw back his head and laughed, "I was trying out new shoes when I spotted you. I left everything and ran to catch you. Excuse me," he said, "I'll be back in a minute." She followed him and stood outside the shop, while he went inside and returned wearing his sandals.

He could see she was upset about something. "Let's sit somewhere and talk, Renee. I have plenty of time. Tell me about yourself. It's been a long time since we last met. You must be married….."

"…….Yes," she interrupted him, "and the mother of two wonderful boys. The younger one is naughty like you." He could detect a gleam in her eyes and he saw she was smiling. "But marriage is tough, Sacchu," she continued, "It's all so different from the fun we had as children. People can be so hurtful."

He could barely hear her in the jostling crowd; he held her elbow and gently steered her towards a Coffee Shop close by. When they were seated at a table for two, the waiter appeared and asked for their order. He asked for four samosas and two cups of Espresso coffee. He knew both were her favourites. While they waited, he told her he had completed his engineering and worked for a private firm in Delhi.

"I'm married, Renee!" he said, smiling, "to a lovely girl called Poonam. We have a five year old son called Ishan. He's quite a handful and makes his mother run all over the house."

"Just like his father," she said with a smile, the dimple back on her right cheek. He was relieved to see her relaxing, but could not help noticing her loss of confidence, and her hesitant speech. She was eating the samosas, dipping them in the ketchup quietly, with downcast eyes. He could not bear to see the sadness she was trying so hard to hide.

"And what about you Renee? How have you been?" he inquired, taking a sip of his coffee.

It was ages since anyone had shown the slightest interest in her feelings: she had begun to feel so alone. Her life with the Varmas was like living with strangers; she felt no connection with anyone in the family, except her sons. While Renee longed for love and understanding, she wondered if Rajdeep was even aware of her innermost needs. Or was it that he no longer had any time for her in his successful and extremely busy life?

"Tell me what your problem is," said Sacchu with concern . "We'll find a way out. For now, come with me to Anita's flat in Southern Avenue."

He paid the bill, and she picked up her bags, and together they walked towards Chowringhee Road. There were taxis waiting in a row, and they sat in the first one, and he gave the driver his sister Anita's address in Southern Avenue. Renee turned towards Sacchu remembering their runaway adventure, when they were searching for her treasure in Varanasi.

"You owe me a ride," she reminded him. "I hope you have money this time. I paid all of five rupees to the rickshaw driver, who took us back to school from Kashi Vatika."

He laughed. "So you have not forgotten!"

"How could I? You tricked me into going without a penny in your pocket."

"We were kids, Renee, with the guts of young children. Life requires more than guts to be lived..."

"Like what...?"she interrupted him impatiently.

"Like," he paused, thinking, "making compromises and adjustments; at times, one has to be willing to surrender and accept defeat, in order to win the larger battle. And yet, one has to keep moving forward... it's the only way."

Renee stared at her friend with new found respect. She smiled and said, "Sacchu, you never fail to surprise me! Such profound wisdom, at your age! You're right...life is full of challenges."

"...for all of us, Renee. One has to learn to get along in society too, and discover one's own path."

"You sound very practical," she commented wryly. She was irritated, by what she recognized to be the truth, in her friend's words; she wished she could be more practical herself, when the need arose for it.

They had reached Southern Avenue, and Sacchu paid the driver the fare. The security guard opened the gate, and let them inside the grounds of the six storied apartment building in which Anita and her family lived. Sacchu noticed Renee lost in deep thought, walking slowly towards one of the lifts in the lobby. He quickly ran up the staircase, yelling, "Race you up to the fourth floor."

He was gone in a flash and she chased him, thankful he had picked up her larger, heavier bag from the taxi when alighting, and she only had her purse to carry. They raced up the steps, going around bends, and past startled residents waiting for the lifts to arrive. She was intent only on beating him, so she gathered her dupatta tightly around her waist and ran ahead. Sacchu slowed his run, hiding at the bends, pretending to be tired, so she would win. She reached the fourth floor and stood there gasping for breath, as he lumbered up slowly.

"You won," he said, "Wow! You sure can run fast."

She scowled at him. "Don't pretend Sacchu! You deliberately lost the race and let me win." He stared at her in mock surprise.

He rang the door bell of his sister's flat, long and hard.

The door was flung open and an irritated Anita peered out, her afternoon nap disturbed by the insistent ringing of the doorbell. She spotted her brother but did not recognize the young woman with him.

"Look who's here Anita!" he exclaimed, ushering Renee inside the flat.

Anita stared for a moment, then cried out in delight, "It's Renee! What a pleasant surprise! What are you doing in Calcutta?"

"My father was posted in Calcutta for many years and we lived in three Railway Colonies here, the last one being at Lakeview Park in Alipore. After retirement they shifted to Lucknow. My husband has his home in Alipore, so I live here too."

"That's wonderful!" exclaimed Anita, happy to hear this bit of news from her old school friend, "We can meet often, Renee... please sit. I'll get some tea."

Anita welcomed her warmly to her home, and they chatted for a while over tea and snacks, while Sacchu went to his room. It was six o'clock already and Anita got busy preparing dinner for all of them. Her eight year old daughter Aarti had come home after playing with her friends downstairs, and Renee was happy to meet her and inquired about her school and class friends. Anita's husband, Suresh, returned around seven thirty, and there was another round of introductions as he met Renee. An hour later, Anita announced that dinner had been served and the hungry gathering enjoyed the delicious aloo gobi and matar paneer served with salad and hot parathas. Everyone relished the food and once dinner was over, Anita went to the fridge and brought out a large bowl of rasgullas of which everyone had two each. Anita's husband retired for the night to their bedroom and her daughter Aarti lingered for a while till she began to feel sleepy. She said goodnight to everyone and went to bed. Renee would be sleeping in her room tonight, but for now, the three childhood friends wanted to sit in the drawing room and talk.

Renee confided to her friends about the deep insecurities she had begun to feel as she grew into a young woman: she had hoped marriage to Rajdeep would give her the sense of security she had been looking for, but events proved to be otherwise. In spite of him earning well, and getting to live in a large, well to do home, she was not happy. Her greatest joy were her two boys. She was beginning to feel alienated from her husband; he no longer paid her any attention and he was hardly ever there for her when she turned to him for emotional support.

She turned towards Anita with an anguished cry, "Could my suffering have anything to do with my childhood trauma of having been left alone as a child for more than a year?"

"Left alone?" exclaimed Anita, shocked that something like this could have happened to Renee.

"Yes!" continued Renee passionately. "And Jatin was with me; he was only ten months old at that time. This is a family secret that is never mentioned by anyone....not even by my father and *Mamoni*."

"Why did your parents leave you?" inquired Anita, sitting taut on the edge of the sofa. "This is too confusing!" she shook her head incredulously, "Tell us exactly what happened. You mentioned you were left alone with Jatin, as a little girl. With whom did you stay?"

Sacchu inquired angrily, "What was so important that made your parents leave their two small kids behind?"

"First things first," said Anita, taking charge like the old times in Manduadih. "Where did they go?"

"United States of America," replied Renee.

"You mean that big country, so far away. Why didn't they take you with them?"

"Frankly, I have no idea. I never asked them. My father received some kind of a scholarship meant only for husband and wife. That meant we had to be left behind with an Uncle and his family, where we stayed during the entire period they were away."

In a steady voice, Renee told her friends, that her father had been awarded the Dwight D. Eisenhower Scholarship to Harvard Business School in 1954 to study a course in management. She had never understood why it was decided that father should accept such a scholarship, in the first place. All his other colleagues had refused to consider the offer, because their children were too small to be left behind. She had been three and a half years old and Jatin a baby of ten months. Renee had learnt from her mother that when they went to Boston they were put up in small apartments, along with other couples, who had come from different countries for the same course on scholarships. It was meant to foster goodwill and understanding among people. Renee knew in her heart, that even if her mother had protested vehemently against the decision to separate her from her children, nobody would have listened to her.

"I must have missed *Mamoni* terribly, Anita!" cried Renee. "I must have run from room to room, looking for her. Why had she left me and gone away so suddenly? Was she angry with me? Would I ever see her again?"

There was pin drop silence in the room.

Renee took a sip of water and continued, "I think it made me a very insecure person. I've spent all my life trying to feel safe but it never seems to happen. Outwardly, I can be strong and capable, but inside I'm still that frightened little girl, searching for her mother."

Sacchu couldn't help thinking that Renee must have wondered where her parents had disappeared. Would they ever return? Where had they gone? Did they miss Jatin and her, and whether they loved them at all? So many questions, from a four year old girl, and no one to give any answers.

Anita stood up, "I'm hungry. Let's have some tea and biscuits." She rose and went into the kitchen to boil some water and make tea.

Renee noticed the sadness in Sacchu's eyes. "Everything will be fine, Sacchu. I'll be happy again, I promise you that."

"Never give up, Renee. That's what life is all about," he said. "It's only by living that one finds the light. One has to keep going forward to triumph in life."

Renee smiled, "Give me a high five Sacchu!", she said, and he did. She continued, "My friend, you are wise beyond your years. I'll keep your words in mind."

Sacchu had rung up Rajdeep from Lindsay Street, having taken his phone number from Renee, asking him not to worry, that she was with him and that she would be spending the night at his sister's house. Next morning, Anita got busy preparing a breakfast of aloo puri for everyone, and packing the tiffin box for her daughter's school lunch. After her husband had left for work, and Aarti went off to school, Anita suggested to Renee that the three of them should meet Rajdeep for lunch and talk things over.

They met around noon at a popular restaurant in Park Street. Rajdeep had taken leave from office and was the first to arrive and occupied a table for four and ordered a cold drink while he waited for the others to arrive. They came fifteen minutes later, and Renee waved on seeing her husband and went to join him, while Sacchu and Anita followed her. She made the introductions, and Rajdeep shook hands with Sacchu, and greeted Anita with a namaste. Rajdeep ordered vegetable pakoras and soft drinks for the others. When the waiter went to get their food and drinks, he came straight to the point.

"Why did you leave home without informing anyone, Renee? That was not a very nice thing to do, the way you walked out, just like that. I was worried sick, till Sacchu called to say you were with him."

"It's not as simple as that, Rajdeep," replied Renee, "It's about me and my feelings. I feel as if you don't want me around any longer. You never seem to have any time for me these days. I crave for attention from you when you come home in the evenings, yet you are always concerned about other things."

Rajdeep was taken aback by her direct accusation. He had never imagined that she had begun to feel so alone, that she would need to walk out of her house one day. He wanted to make amends, and reassured her that he would work to make her happy again.

"I care for you in my own way," he said. He bit thoughtfully into an onion pakora, "What is the way forward?" he asked.

"She goes back with you, of course," Anita replied quickly, before Renee could say anything.

Renee shook her head firmly. "No Anita," she said with conviction, "not to that house. I've had enough. I tried my best to adjust to the large household and obviously did not succeed; I feel I am not wanted there any longer. I want to spare myself more misery."

"If 1 may suggest something," interrupted Sacchu,"You should rent another apartment in Calcutta and move out."

Rajdeep stared at him aghast. "Impossible!" he said, "My parents would never agree to such a thing."

Sacchu continued speaking, "It's the only way out. You will be living in the same city in another locality. Look for a decent, two bedroom flat Rajdeep, and move your family out. I live in Delhi in company accommodation with my wife and son. My parents stay in another area in their own small flat. I can go and take care of their needs when required, and they are there to give us support when we need it. It works for both of us."

Anita nodded, while Rajdeep seemed to ponder Sacchu's suggestion. Renee was relieved and happy that Sacchu had come to her rescue yet again, by suggesting a way out of the awful situation she found herself in. "There is a lot of sense in what Sacchu is suggesting," agreed Anita. "Talk to your parents. They'll come around and accept the idea in due course. It's best for Renee. She'll have her own home."

"We'll think about it," said Rajdeep, as the waiter arrived with their food. They had ordered Chinese food and the waiter laid out the noodles and fried rice and other dishes on the table. The four of them enjoyed their meal and chatted amiably. They ate so much that nobody wanted any dessert except Sacchu who had a chocolate ice cream, while the others had coffee.

Rajdeep paid the bill and rose from the table. "Let's go home, Renee," he said, "The boys are waiting for you."

"So am I Rajdeep," she replied, "I took this step for them too, after a lot of deliberation. I want them to grow up with a happy mother."

The four of them parted at the entrance of the restaurant. As usual, Park Street was buzzing with activity with shoppers, and the office crowd out for a quick lunch, milling on the pavements. Renee felt a ray of hope as she bid goodbye to Sacchu, and asked him to give her love to his wife and son. She hugged Anita, and the two of them promised to meet again sometime soon. Rajdeep had walked ahead and she followed him with quickened steps and a hopeful heart.

CHAPTER 14

MOVING OUT

Rajdeep, Renee and the boys moved into their new flat on the second floor of a seven storey building on Lord Sinha Road. Rajdeep had contacted a broker and visited quite a few apartments, before finalizing this one, and paying the advance rent. He liked the location and the fact that the occupants included many young families like theirs. His sons would have children their age to play with, and school was not too far away. The boys were excited to hear about the shift because it meant that they would be able to make plenty of friends in their very own building. Rajdeep's parents did not take well to the idea, at first. *Bauji* was silent on the issue, and did not argue with his younger son; the scars of his earlier battle with Ashok ran deep. Besides, he was growing old and did not have the energy or the will to counter Rajdeep's decision. He did his best to find out what had prompted this sudden move but found, to his dismay, that Rajdeep was unwilling to even discuss the topic. *Bauji* sensed his mood and let him do as he wished.

When Rajdeep first broke the news, over breakfast, to his mother, her face turned dark with anger. She said nothing, but looked pointedly at her daughter-in-law; so Renee was now taking her son away from them. She will never succeed, she thought to herself, I will make sure of that. She decided not to argue with Rajdeep as she did not wish to antagonize her son. However, her mood turned surly as the details of the move began to be discussed. She spoke roughly to Renee, and that too only when required: she had not yet forgiven her for walking out of the house abruptly without so much as taking her permission or having the courtesy to inform her. Instead, when her son had gone to fetch her, she had returned on the condition that they move out of the Alipore house. Her beautiful house! With all the comforts and luxuries any one could wish for. On her part, Renee spoke little to anyone. She wished things could have been sorted out more amicably, and they could have continued to live together; she had tried her best to adjust to the family, but clearly that was not enough, and it had become imperative for them to move out.

The truck came on a Sunday morning and loading began after breakfast. There wasn't much stuff, so it was all done by lunchtime. When lunch was announced by Bansi, Abhishek and Gaurav, who until then had been supervising the loading of the furniture, went running towards the dining room and were promptly stopped in their tracks by their mother.

"Wash your hands, they're dirty," she said.

"They're clean Mummy," protested Abhishek.

"And we're very hungry," added Gaurav. "Our hands are not dirty at all."

"Show me," ordered Renee. Quickly, they upturned their grubby palms to show dirt and bits of hay sticking to it.

They looked at each other, then raced to the bathroom to wash them clean.

Over lunch, *Bauji* did not speak much and Ma kept staring at her plate in silence, eating little. Rajdeep kept the conversation going, by promising to look up his parents, as soon as they were settled in their new flat. They would all be coming for lunch every Sunday, he added brightly. Renee was relieved to hear the boys prattling to *Bauji* about playing cricket and football with all the new friends they would be making in their new home. Lunch over, it was time to leave. *Bauji*, Ma and the house helps stood in the verandah and waved to them as Rajdeep, Renee and the kids drove away in their new Fiat car.

It was tough in the beginning, being on their own; everyone had to pitch in. The two part-time maids Renee had employed, came twice a day to do their work. Renee worked hard to improve her culinary skills, reading cook books and trying out new recipes, while her sons were thrilled to be living in a multi-storied building for the first time. With their parents occupied in adjusting the furniture and putting up new curtains, Abhishek and Gaurav ran off to the lobby on the ground floor to make new friends. Every evening, after finishing their homework and drinking their glass of milk and Bournvita, they would rush down to play in the small playground within the premises, which had a swing, a slide and a jungle gym. A brick colored boundary wall enclosed the grounds, and there was a security guard present at all times at the gate.

Once the house had been settled, Renee started going downstairs in the evenings to sit on the wooden benches, waiting for Rajdeep to return from work. She made friends with the other mothers who were there along with their kids. Among them was Manvi, a well-dressed, attractive woman whose son Ayush, aged six was Gaurav's friend. He had an older sister, Nikita aged eight. The women discussed many current topics, including the latest fashion trends, filmy gossip and sometimes exchanged recipes. Renee marvelled at the bravado of the other ladies; she, herself, did not speak much and was hesitant to express her own opinion. Her vivacious, easy going confidence had all but disappeared. The years she had spent in the Alipore house had had a demoralizing effect on Renee; these days she was never very sure about anything.

One would have thought that once Rajdeep and Renee were in their own flat, they would draw closer to each other, as they had been in the initial years of their marriage, but this did not happen. Rajdeep did his bit around the house: shopping for grocery on weekends, fixing gadgets and other things that needed his attention. He would be gone for long hours on Saturdays and other holidays to spend time with his parents, and help *Bauji* with the accounts of the Liluah factory. Abhishek and Gaurav often accompanied him to their grandparents house. When she complained she was lonely, he said that *Bauji* and Ma were getting on in years, and he wished to do his duty by them. Renee had hoped that this move would cement her marriage: the exact opposite happened. In his heart Rejdeep blamed her for driving him away from his parents. He never said so in words, but she felt his rejection and this added to her feeling of insecurity..

Kunal had got married to a girl of his mother's choice from Lucknow. He had waited till his sister Ragini was married and settled in her new life. Immediately after that, Mrs. Kamla Chopra had taken it upon herself to look for a suitable girl for her elder son, and she soon found a girl she approved of, called Manvi. After their wedding Kunal and Manvi left for Calcutta. He had shifted from his small apartment in New Alipore to a three bedroom one on the fifth floor of a seven storey building on Lord Sinha Road. He and his new bride had got busy furnishing and decorating their new home. He had enjoyed showing Manvi around Calcutta, and introducing her to his friends. It was not long before Manvi was pregnant and they were expecting their first child. They were overjoyed to be parents of a beautiful baby girl, whom they named Nikita. When their daughter was two years old, their son Ayush was born. Kunal had felt a sense of completeness he had never felt before, as he cradled his son in his protective arms. He stared in wonder at his sleepy face and decided he was going to make him into a strong and caring man like himself. Unmindful of his father's future planning, Ayush had stretched languorously, yawned and promptly gone back to sleep.

Kunal and Manvi took to the comfortable life Calcutta offered the young professional and his family in the seventies: there was the swinging music and food hub in Park Street, shopping in New Market, and the active and exciting Club scene. Kunal had resigned from Lakeview Club as it was too far from his new house, and was looking out to joining one of the better ones which offered varied sporting and other facilities.

Manvi and Renee's children met in the playground within their complex and soon Gaurav and Ayush were inseparable, busy planning their next escapade. One evening, a few months after they had moved in, Renee remembered Gaurav had a Hindi test the next day and she had promised to help him prepare for it. She went looking for him downstairs, and not finding him there, decided to check at Manvi's flat. When she rang the doorbell, her friend opened the door.

"Oh, It's you Renee! What a pleasant surprise!" Manvi greeted her warmly. She opened her door wide, "Come in, come in...."

"Is Gaurav at your place?" Renee inquired, still standing outside.

"No," replied Manvi, shaking her head, "Why? What's the matter?"

"He has his Hindi test tomorrow and needs to study," replied Renee in a concerned voice. "I want to sit with him and help him revise."

"Let him play a while more," said Manvi, laughing. "They must all be in someone else's house kicking up a ruckus, no doubt. You come in, and we can chat a bit."

Renee stepped inside, a bit hesitantly. She saw it was a well appointed home, tastefully done with beautiful curios and a large painting on the wall behind the sofa. Asking her to take a seat, Manvi went to the kitchen and returned with two glasses of chilled Coke. The two of them were soon having an animated discussion on the rising vegetable prices. Renee liked Manvi; she was open and genuine.

It was past six o'clock when the doorbell rang. Manvi opened the door, to let her husband in, and Renee nearly fell off the sofa. She spilled some of the Coke on her kurta, and hastily tried to wipe it off with her handkerchief. The distinguished looking man who entered, holding a dark brown leather briefcase, was Kunal. She saw his mop of thick hair had started greying; the salt and pepper made him look more mature. How many years had gone by since they had met in Park Street and he had dropped her home in the rain? She had seen life at close quarters since then and, it seemed, so had he. The familiar looking face was stronger, harder; he strode in, and placed his brief case on the dining table. He found his wife had a visitor and, not wishing to disturb them, he asked her to bring him his tea in the bedroom.

Even though he pretended not to, Kunal had recognized Renee instantly. He was dismayed at the change in her: older and well dressed, no doubt, but a sadder version of the vivacious, bright eyed girl he had known in Lakeview Park. He was aware she had married Rajdeep and moved into his spacious family home in Alipore. After that he had not heard from either of them. What had happened in these intervening years to lessen the glow, to dim the sparkle in her eyes? What had Rajdeep done to her? More importantly, what had Renee done to herself? Kunal knew it was a matter of choices; what seemed the best option at the time, could go very wrong; one spent the rest of one's life setting things right. He himself was largely a self-made man; he knew it was in Renee's hands to straighten out whatever was wrong in her life.

CHAPTER 15

GOOD FRIENDS

Rajdeep's job was rewarding and he took care of his family; at the same time, making sure he did not neglect his elderly parents. With advancing age, *Bauji* had stopped going to the Liluah factory altogether. He had entrusted it's day to day management to the same trusted officers and workers they had employed many years ago; in any case, it was running much below it's capacity due to reduced demand for the once popular Ambassador cars. Rajdeep had started going to Alipore on Saturday evenings to help his father with the accounts, and since it was late in the evening by the time they finished, he usually had dinner with them before returning home. His mother made sure Bansi cooked his favorite dishes. Back in their apartment in Lord Sinha Road, Renee put the children to bed early, and watched her favourite serials as she ate her dinner alone.

Sundays were meant for family outings and the boys would be excited about it from the morning. This was one day they finished their milk to the last drop at one go. Rajdeep usually drove to Victoria Memorial or the Maidan and parked his car on the right side of the wide road. Abhishek and Gaurav ran out into the vast expanse of the open space, while their parents tried to catch up with them; once they had enjoyed running around, the boys played cricket or football with their father. Renee sat on a small durrie which she would spread on the grass, soaking in the greenery, and watching them play. Tired and hungry, they would drive to Park Street to have lunch in one of the many restaurants there. These were precious moments for Renee when Rajdeep gave them his undivided attention: it made up for other days, when she felt lonely and neglected.

Once a month, the family went for lunch on Sunday to the Alipore house. The boys loved it, and after greeting their Dada and Dadi, went out to the large back lawn to play. *Bauji's* walk had slowed down and the old fire and enthusiasm were missing. He had aged considerably, and the losses in his business had saddened him further. Ma was still her old self, well turned out, and commander-in-chief of her household. Over the years, she had learned to work around a tightened budget and saw to it that there was no wastage of any kind, be it in the shopping of fruits and vegetables, or the cleaning agents used to wash utensils or wipe the floors of the large two storied house. Renee noticed that Birju, too, had mellowed with age and no longer took pleasure in baiting his mistress; rather, he seemed eager to please her and followed her instructions to the last detail. Mrs. Varma, however, had not forgiven Renee for moving her family out of the large Alipore house, and leaving them alone to fend for themselves. Her behavior towards her daughter-in-law continued to be cold and unfriendly. Rajdeep's sister Pinky naturally sided with her parents. On her visits with her family, she played with her nephews but barely acknowledged Renee's presence, leave alone, show any affection. She blamed her sister-in-law for breaking up the family.

Renee's sense of alienation was largely due to the fact that the insecure child in her was frightened, and needed a warm hug, and someone to hold her securely in his arms and tell her she was safe. She was a prisoner of her circumstances; she was unable to break the barriers she had built around herself. The more she needed love, the more she succeeded in driving off people around her.

The truth was Renee craved for love. She was painfully reminded of how alone she had become, one Sunday afternoon, when they visited the Varma's for lunch. She had been up early in the morning doing the dishes, fixing breakfast, and laying the beds because both her part-time maids had taken leave for the day. She got Abhishek and Gaurav to help, and they willingly ran around the house, running errands for her. She washed the clothes and hung them out to dry in the balcony. By the time they reached the Varma's house around noon, Renee was feeling exhausted and decided to take rest in the guest room downstairs. She fell asleep as soon as she lay on the bed; when she woke up, and looked at her watch, it was past three in the afternoon. She jumped up, straightened out her sari, combed her hair and rushed to the dining room, only to find it deserted. Lunch was over: a plate lay neatly upturned on a place mat, katori and spoon by it's side. Cold food in covered bowls was placed in front of it. Although Renee felt deeply hurt, she had no other option but to swallow her pride, and eat her lunch alone because she was very hungry. She sat down and helped herself to the cold dal, mutton curry, fried bhindi, salad and rice.

Rajdeep came in, looking for a glass of water. Renee put down her spoon and rose, saying accusingly, "Rajdeep! You didn't call me when everyone was eating lunch."

"You never asked me to," he replied, shrugging his shoulders, and pouring water from a stainless steel jug into a glass. "When I peeped in at one thirty, you were fast asleep."

"Why didn't you wake me up?" she asked, a sharp, anxious edge to her voice.

"So, it's always my fault! Never yours. Everyone else is to blame, except you. Grow up Renee! You no longer have any choice but to adjust."

He had finished drinking water and turned and walked out of the room to join the others in the back verandah, where afternoon coffee had just been ordered. Renee ate her food in silence.

Even after they reached home, she thought it prudent not to raise the topic with Rajdeep. There was never any point in arguing with him these days; there were times when he was a complete stranger to her. Renee had been unprepared for this aspect of his personality. During his courtship days, when they used to meet in the Lakeview Club, he had been very courteous and eager to please her. His attitude towards her had changed gradually, but now the neglect of her feelings had made her withdraw into a shell; she had nobody to turn to for support. She had met Anita a few times, who encouraged her to think of taking up a teaching job. Anita had recently begun accompanying her daughter to school, where she taught in the nursery section. Renee was beginning to feel empty inside, and the simple things which gave her joy once, no longer did. She went through her household chores mechanically, lost in thought of happier days gone by. Abhishek and Gaurav were growing up fine, and looking after them kept her busy. She prayed to God to show her the way to a life of greater personal happiness.

One fine day, Gaurav invited his friend Ayush to accompany them to the Maidan on the coming Sunday for a game of cricket, without bothering to inform his parents about it. Ayush said he would only come if his sister came along too, so the invitation was extended to her also; neither of the two boys thought it necessary to seek their parent's permission. Next Sunday, as she served a breakfast of buttered toast and scrambled eggs, Renee noticed Gaurav fidgeting with his food and whispering something to his brother eagerly, who tried his best to ignore him.

"What is it Gaurav? You don't like the toast ?" asked his mother sharply.

"No Mummy, it's nice. I like it," replied her younger son, innocence writ large on his face. He bent his head and dipped one piece of the toast in the ketchup and began making a pattern on the plate.

"Eat it!" ordered his mother, losing her cool.

 Meanwhile, in her flat, Manvi was grateful that Ayush did not fuss over breakfast; he drank his milk at one go, and finished his omellete and toast without prompting. He put away his plate in the kitchen sink, quickly took his towel and ran for a bath. Nikita went to her room to get ready. Kunal was relaxing with the morning newspaper over a cup of coffee and he watched in amazement as his daughter squatted on the floor and tied her brother's shoe laces, something she had always resented being told to do. What could the two be up to? They went to the kitchen where their mother was busy emptying the fridge she had defrosted early that morning, in order to clean it. They filled their water bottles with drinking water, and stood innocently before her.

"Can we go to Gaurav's house to play?" asked Ayush.

"Why, of course!" she answered distractedly, placing left overs, fruits and vegetables on the kitchen counter.

"Kunal!" she shouted to her husband, as the children left for Gaurav'house. "Please come and help me wash these...I can't clean the fridge by myself." Kunal finished his coffee, slowly folded the newspaper he had been reading, and reluctantly walked towards the kitchen to lend his wife a helping hand.

Their phone rang insistently and he went back to the drawing room to answer it. It was Rajdeep telling him not to worry, that Nikita and Ayush would be safe with them on the outing.

"Hey, wait a minute!" Kunal replied incredulously, "What outing are you talking about?"

"Didn't they tell you?" asked Rajdeep, surprised. "They are coming with us to the Maidan for some cricket practice."

Kunal cupped his hands on the receiver, and yelled at his wife, "Manvi! Did you give the children permission to go out today with Gaurav and his family?"

She stopped midway and stared at him askance, the soap solution from the sponge dripping on the floor and making a small puddle. Hastily, she threw the wet sponge into the kitchen sink. "What?" she asked angrily, "Are they claiming I did?"

"It's Rajdeep asking if they can go with them," he explained.

"O.K." she said dismissively, "Please come and help me clean up this mess."

Kunal spoke on the phone. "It's fine, Rajdeep, the kids can go with you. I only hope they aren't too much trouble."

"Don't worry," said Rajdeep, " In any case they'll be busy playing."

"Manvi and I plan to have lunch at the Tollygunge Club today. Why don't you bring the kids there and join us for a meal?"

"Don't take so much trouble. We'll reach the kids and go somewhere else for lunch," replied Rajdeep but Kunal would have none of it. He insisted they should eat together, and eventually Rajdeep agreed to meet him there around one o'clock.

Kunal and Manvi left for Tollygunge Club around twelve thirty, the fridge having been duly cleaned and restarted. It being a Sunday, there was not much traffic on the roads and they soon entered the Tolly Club gates and drove up the tree lined driveway. Kunal parked his car in the allotted area and they walked up to the tables and garden chairs which had been spread out for members and their families to sit and relax under shady trees; the ground was pebbled to avoid slush and mud during the rains. Beyond, was a wide expanse of beautiful, green lawns which served as the Golf course; they could see eager players teeing off with caddies in tow. In the far distance, one could see the green woods, almost a mini forest amidst the metro city of Calcutta.

Once they were seated, a bearer appeared, to take their order. Kunal ordered a beer for himself and a soft drink for Manvi. He looked at his watch and saw it was almost one o'clock. "The children must be hungry, Kunal," said Manvi in a concerned voice. "Why are they delaying?"

"They'll be here soon," he said, taking a sip of the beer. He had left word at the gate that he was expecting guests and to let them inside.

Ten minutes later, they heard shouts of joy, and saw Nikita and Ayush waving and running towards them, followed by Abhishek and Gaurav. A smiling Rajdeep followed the kids, as Renee tried her best to keep up with all of them.

Ayush ran straight into his mother's outstretched arms, and gave her a tight hug, "I missed you Mom!"

"So did I," she said, "Did you have fun?"

"Yes, lots!" he replied.

Kunal got busy welcoming his guests, and fetching chairs for everyone to sit. The children decided to explore the grounds and the adults were left to themselves. It was the first time Rajdeep was meeting Manvi and he liked her immediately: she seemed friendly and easy going.

"I hear you come from Lucknow," he remarked, taking a sip of the cold beer which the waiter had brought. "How do you like Calcutta?"

"I like it now," she replied, "... I find the people very warm and friendly."

"*Free time mein New Market ghoomti rehti hai!*" Kunal said laughingly.

"Not true!" objected Manvi. "Yes, I do like wandering in all the lanes; the sheer variety of shops and goods available is dazzling. It's my favorite shopping place, no doubt."

"And you, Renee," asked Kunal, turning to her, "do you also

like going to New Market?"

She ignored his query completely, and turning towards Manvi, asked her details about some school function Gaurav had been talking about. Kunal could see she was tense and unhappy. She was behaving as though this was the first time she was meeting him: there had been no Lakeview Park, no taxi ride in the rain, no meetings in the Maidan. He tried offering her the chips, which she refused politely, turning her face away. He could feel her rejecting his friendship, and he was puzzled by her behavior, while Renee did her best to hide her pain from Kunal. At twenty, she had been headstrong, and sure of herself, and made her choices believing them to be right at the time. Life had taught her many lessons and the Blue team Captain had been battered emotionally. Her confidence was broken into tiny little pieces. Who was there to help her put it back? Why should Kunal bother about her? He had his own family and she was happy to see he was a devoted husband and father. Renee did not want either his pity or his sympathy.

Their plates of golden brown fried fish and fried chicken arrived and the children came running back.

"Come on, all of you," said Manvi, rising from her chair, "We're going to the washroom to clean your dirty hands. You've been playing all day."

"No Mama," protested Ayush, "See, they're clean." He upturned his palms to show dirt sticking in all corners. Kunal laughed, "Let them eat….they must be hungry."

"No way!" insisted his wife, rising and leading all the children into the main Club house, where the washrooms were located.

"All right," said Kunal, "We'll wait for you."

Food was delicious and everyone enjoyed their meal. Afterwards, the children wanted ice cream and they walked up to the ice cream counter to order their choice of flavours.

"This Club is very good, Kunal," said Rajdeep, licking his chocolate cone. "I need to ask my company for a corporate membership; I know a few guys whom they have sponsored."

"In that case, you should apply immediately. It takes time to process the applications and let me warn you, there will be a formal interview for Renee and you."

"Hope we can get through it," smiled Rajdeep. "But, seriously, this is such a wonderful place to bring the kids on weekends. I could even start playing golf."

They had been walking towards the car park and said their goodbyes before going home. Rajdeep and Renee thanked their hosts for an enjoyable afternoon and walked towards their car. Once the boys were safely seated, Rajdeep drove out of the Tolly Club gates, followed closely by his friend Kunal and his family. Renee and Kunal did not have the slightest inkling at that time, that their lives were going to be intertwined again, in the most unexpected of ways.

CHAPTER 16

LOVE IS A MANY SPLENDOURED THING

March and April were busy months for the children of the residential complex, as they began preparing for their annual examinations. Once the exams were over, and the holiday homework given out, it was early May and the heat in the daytime was getting oppressive. Much to the children's delight, the schools began closing for the long awaited summer holidays. Rajdeep left with his family for his home town for a two week visit. Ayush missed his friend Gaurav; he accompanied his sister downstairs for some exercise and fresh air in the evenings, but many of his friends were away, and he merely sat on the jungle gym watching other youngsters playing. The Varmas returned from their vacation on Sunday morning, and that evening Ayush insisted that his parents visit them so he could play with Gaurav.

Rajdeep opened the door, and was surprised to see that Kunal and Manvi, accompanied by Ayush, had come for a visit and welcomed them warmly into his home. His elder son Abhishek had gone to meet his friends and Nikita preferred to stay at home and read her latest Enid Blyton book. He called out to his younger son, "Look who's here!" Gaurav came running to meet Ayush and the two embraced with screams of delight, like two long lost comrades, who had been forcibly parted. They ran to the children's room to pull out their favourite engine set and got busy laying out the tracks. The others took their seats in the drawing room and Rajdeep threw open the windows to let in some cool air. The whirring fan was circulating the hot, humid air inside the room. Calcutta waited eagerly for the pre-monsoon showers, of which, as yet, there was no sign. Renee was in the kitchen getting the atta dough ready for making chapattis for dinner, spreading out the flour in a round, open dish, adding the water slowly, to get the right consistency of the dough. She was giving it a good pounding with both hands when the doorbell rang, and she heard Kunal's voice, along with others. She put the ready dough in a covered dish and put it away in the fridge for later use.

Renee emerged from the kitchen, wiping the sweat from her forehead, and walked hurriedly to the bathroom, splashed cool water on her face, wiped it dry with a towel and combed her hair. She adjusted her sari pallu, put on a maroon bindi and returned to the kitchen. In a few minutes, she emerged carrying two plates of home-made snacks: shakkarpara and nimki. She greeted her guests, and placed the tray on the centre table.

"Would you like some coffee or tea? Or something cold?" she asked Kunal and Manvi.

"I'd like some coffee, if it's not too much trouble," said Manvi, smiling at her friend.

"I'll have a cup too," requested Rajdeep. He turned towards Kunal, "What about you?"

"Water, please," said Kunal. He had suddenly lost all appetite for food or drink; he did not like the way Renee was looking, nor the way she slowly went about her household chores. Her eyes were swollen and her face ever so slightly puffed up, as though the pain she was trying hard to hide, had taken its toll on her beauty. Renee took out some of the snacks in two stainless steel bowls and went to the children's bedroom to give it to the kids, before going back to the kitchen to make some coffee.

Manvi took a few of the nimkis on a quarter plate and ate one piece. "These are delicious!" she exclaimed.

"Home made," said Rajdeep proudly, "by our family cook in my village."

Renee came and sat on a single seater, listening quietly to the others in the room while they talked. Rajdeep and Manvi had much to talk about, and she insisted on telling them the latest gossip doing the rounds among the residents of their building. Kunal looked at Renee, pale and withdrawn, sitting silently in a corner, and he felt a stab of pain in his chest.

He saw his wife had finished her coffee and rose, calling out to his son, "Ayush! It is getting late……you both have school tomorrow." He turned towards Rajdeep, "You guys must have a lot of unpacking to do after a long trip. We won't disturb you any further." He did not even look at Renee, as he walked briskly out of the main door, and pressed the elevator button to go home.

In the coming months, life took on a predictable pattern for the Varmas and the Chopras. The men went to work, the children to their respective schools, and the two wives tried to make the most of their long days at home. There were the weekend outings their children eagerly looked forward to.

Rajdeep took his family once a month to his parent's house for Sunday lunch. They still went to the Maidan to enjoy the open spaces and the boys took their ball along for some football practice. Kunal almost always took his family to the Tollygunge Club; for him Sunday meant a beer followed by good food, and his family enjoyed the outing too.

A few months later, as Kunal was getting out of his car one evening, Abhishek came running to him. "Kunal uncle! Kunal uncle" he cried excitedly, "Ayush and Gaurav had a fight... Gaurav climbed on to the swing first and Ayush also wanted to go..."

"What happened...?" Kunal put his hand on Abhishek's shoulder and asked him gently.

The words came tumbling out. "A girl was on the other swing and these two were fighting to go on this one. Gaurav climbed on first and started swinging...Ayush was very angry... he picked up a stone and threw it at him. Gaurav got hurt on the forehead and is bleeding badly."

"Where is he?" Kunal asked, concerned by what he had heard.

"There!" pointed Abhishek towards a gulmohur tree on one side of the playground, under which Renee was standing, holding the injured Gaurav, and pressing her handkerchief on to the wound to stop the blood flow. Kunal strode up and taking out his handkerchief, replaced the one she had been pressing on to it. He saw the wound had dried up and blood was caked over it. The boy needed to be taken immediately to a hospital, and he knew Rajdeep was out of town on official work; he grabbed Gaurav's hand and, pushing the excited children around him to make way, ran with him to his car.

"I'm taking him to hospital, Renee!" he shouted, as he made Gaurav sit on the passenger seat next to him, and drove off. He saw Renee standing forlornly under the gulmohur tree, holding on to her elder son's hand.

In the Emergency Room, the Doctor on duty examined Gaurav, and told Kunal that since the wound was not deep, it did not require any stitches. He prescribed an anti-tetanus injection and a course of antibiotics, and asked the nurse to clean and dress the wound. As he wrote out the prescription he told Kunal, "Bring him back after two days to change the dressing. Please ensure that it remains absolutely dry. And don't send him to school for a few days." Kunal went straight to the hospital Pharmacy to buy the prescribed medicine. As he was walking out of the hospital, he felt someone tug at his trousers; he stopped to find it was Gaurav, wanting to hold his hand. He smiled and let him clutch his dirty little fingers around his: comforted, the boy held on tightly as they walked back to the car park.

Renee and Abhishek were sitting on the building steps, waiting for them; Kunal handed Renee the prescription and medicines, and told her what the doctor had advised. The elevator had stopped and they walked inside, and Gaurav pressed the buttons immediately for their two floors. As Renee stood close to Kunal, her head almost touching his shoulder, she smelt his particular smell of cologne and sweat, and felt the same sense of security she had felt in the heavy rain in Park Street many years ago; she edged closer to him. The lift stopped on the second floor and the doors began sliding open slowly-her sons were the first to get out and run towards their flat and she quickly followed them. When she looked back, the doors had closed and the lift had moved upwards to the next floor.

When Kunal rang the doorbell of his flat, Manvi opened the door and he could tell instantly that she was angry with him. He was exhausted from the extra work in office and the unexpected trip to the hospital: all he wanted was a hot cup of tea.

"Where have you been?" she confronted him immediately. "Nikita has been waiting all evening for you..." Oh God, he thought, I completely forgot....I had promised to take her to the stationery shop to buy material for her art class tomorrow.

He placed his briefcase on the drawing room carpet. "You must have heard from the kids what happened in the playground this evening," he said. "Ayush threw a stone at Gaurav after a fight. It hit him on the forehead and he got badly hurt."

" Yes...Nikita told me. I know he was hurt, but it is not as if Ayush did it on purpose," said Manvi defensively. "Children are bound to fight, Kunal...even best friends."

"Hurting someone physically is unacceptable, Manvi. Under any circumstances. The sooner Ayush understands this, the better for him." He looked around the room. "Where is he?" he asked angrily, "I need to talk to him."

"No!" protested Manvi, "Don't say anything tonight...he's already very upset. He realizes he's done something wrong."

"All right," said Kunal resignedly, picking up his purse and walking towards the door, "I'll take Nikita out to the shop to buy her stuff."

"No need for it now," said Manvi, "She found some old art

material she can use tomorrow in her class. I'll make you some tea. You must be tired." She went to the kitchen and returned after a while with a tray carrying biscuits and two cups of tea, one of which she handed her husband.

She sat on the sofa near him, and took a sip of tea. "I still don't understand," she said thoughtfully, "why you had to take Gaurav to the hospital at all."

Surprised by his wife's comment, and the implicit accusation that he had done something he should not have done, Kunal looked at her sharply. "Please understand," he said, his voice rising, "Gaurav needed immediate medical attention and you know very well Rajdeep is in Bangalore for work."

"It is not as if Renee is all by herself in Calcutta," continued Manvi plaintively. "Her in-laws live in Alipore. She's fought with them and tries to manage everything on her own...it's all her fault! If she had only cared to inform them of the accident, they would have immediately sent their car over, to take Gaurav to the hospital."

"Do you know how long it would have taken for their car to reach here, from Alipore Park Road, in rush hour traffic? At least an hour, if not more." He rose with his cup of tea in his hand and paced about the room; he was disgusted at his wife's logic. "Renee had nothing to do with my decision to take Gaurav to hospital."

"Oh!" exclaimed Manvi, stung at his reply. She rose from the sofa seat. "You don't need to speak up for Renee," she reminded him pointedly, as she went inside the kitchen to start fixing dinner. "The Varmas are mere acquaintances and we should keep our distance from them."

Next morning, while driving to work, Kunal wondered if there was any truth in his wife's accusations that he had been soft towards Renee. As he wove his way through the morning rush hour traffic, he began to think if she had been right after all: where was the need for him to panic and rush the boy to hospital? It was barely two kilometers away and Renee could well have taken him in a taxi. Was it because he was beginning to care for her? He swerved sharply as a bicycle laden with raw bananas appeared suddenly in front of his car. He could not understand the change in Renee, her isolation and consequent loneliness. Kunal wanted to see Renee happy again, facing the world with a spring in her steps and a smile in her heart. With a start he realized that he had reached his office and he had an important meeting barely half an hour later. He must not let himself think of Renee so much.

CHAPTER 17

RENEE AND KUNAL

Rajdeep's membership of the Tollygunge Club came by middle of October, and the family was happy to avail of it's various facilities. Sunday lunch at the Tolly in the winter months offered delights few other places in Calcutta could match. Families sat around tables, even as the sunshine peeped through the leaves of the large shady trees, making speckled patterns on the checked tablecloths. In addition, members could sit in the Wills Shamiana, an open lounge covered with a tiled roof overlooking the golf course on one side where one of the many bars is located. It was early November, and the Club premises were filled with the Sunday crowd, out to make the most of the winter months. Kunal was walking with his family towards the open sitting area when Ayush spotted his friend Gaurav standing under one of the trees with his parents and brother; he raced off to meet him. Gaurav's wound had healed completely with no sign of even a slight scar, and the two were inseparable again.

Rajdeep decided to get wafer chips for the children from the snacks counter at the Wills Shamiana and gestured to Abhishek and Nikita to join him; Manvi followed her daughter. Renee was sitting alone at a table, soaking in the soft, winter sun. On an impulse, Kunal went to sit with her: he noticed how attractive she looked in her yellow kurta and churidar, her shoulder length hair framing her face. All the hard work she did in running her home had toned her body and made her fitter; her stomach had flattened and she had almost regained the figure he had once admired in Lakeview Club. The contours of her face had matured and made her look more beautiful. Motherhood and the intervening years had only added to her appeal. Yet Kunal was sensitive enough to notice that Renee had an insecure look, as if she was searching for something or someone; with his discerning eyes he could see she needed emotional support and was trying hard to hide her pain.

He sat on a chair near her, and came straight to the point. "Let's talk about you Renee," he said, "Have you been to Lakeview Park after your father retired from Railway service, and your parents left Calcutta?"

She shook her head. "It would serve no purpose," she said sadly, "Nobody knows me there now."

From such close proximity, she could see the hair on his chest through the shirt button he had left open, and noticed that it had begun greying. It somehow made him look wiser and stronger. It had a calming effect on her, as if she was sitting with someone who cared for her; she blushed and turned her gaze away from him hastily.

He was looking at her intently. "Do you still read books?" he inquired.

"I've stopped reading completely, Kunal" replied Renee, speaking slowly, measuring her words. "I don't think I can go through an entire book now."

"You must start reading again, Renee," replied Kunal, in his strong voice, full of warmth, "Reading books is so much a part of who you are as a person. Don't cut yourself off from a source of such great happiness…it only adds to your loneliness." He leant forward and asked her, "Tell me the name of one book you've always wanted to read."

"Rebecca," she whispered, "by Daphne du Maurier."

They could see the others returning, carrying food and drinks from the Wills Shamiana. While Abhishek and Nikita were engaged in conversation, eating potato wafers from their packets, the two younger ones were chasing each other, mouth stuffed with chips. Manvi and Rajdeep were watching their steps, trying not to spill the drinks they were carrying. Gaurav came running up to his mother in a sudden outpouring of love, and stuffed a few wafers into her mouth with his grubby hands: chips never tasted so good.

Kunal had risen and was protesting loudly as Rajdeep held out a glass of iced, soft drink to him. "I am not having this!" he announced laughing, "Don't punish me Rajdeep…let's go get a beer."

Kunal was already taking tall strides towards the bar, Rajdeep smiling and trying to catch up with his friend.

It was almost a week before Kunal found the time from his hectic work schedule to visit Oxford Book Store and buy the book, Rebecca by Daphne du Maurier. On the way home, he encountered the usual rush hour traffic, cars honking furiously, trying to edge each other out, two wheelers squeezed in haphazardly, and the swift hand rickshaws weaving in and out and racing ahead. He waited resignedly as the cars in his lane inched forward, and it was a good half an hour before he drove inside their complex gate and parked in his usual place. He spotted Renee in the lobby stepping out for her evening walk.

"Renee!" he called. She looked around and saw him walking briskly towards her, holding his briefcase in one hand and a paper packet in the other.

She stood on the verandah, close to the top most step, and looked at him questioningly. "What is it Kunal?" she asked, as he approached her.

He paused at the lowest step and looked up at her. He saw that she was wearing a white shirt collared kurta, which had half sleeves with upturned cuffs; she had matched it with a bright pink, ikkat salwar. The top button of her kurta had broken off, and she had hurriedly used a safety pin in it's place. Her shoulder length hair was loosely brushed behind her ears and she had put on a maroon bindi on her forehead. Kunal had never seen her look so young and so vulnerable and he had never loved her more. He looked deep into her eyes and she drowned in them, as if she was seeing eternity. Neither could move.

Duty called just at that point of time. She heard Rajdeep calling her from the car park, "Come and help me get these packets out...I bought some fruits for the house."

Kunal handed her the book, "I bought this for you on my way back from office. I hope you are going to read it."

"Thank you," she said softly, as she took the book, and went to join her husband.

From that moment onwards, Renee felt Kunal's love

enveloping her in its protective warmth, and she began to feel safe for the first time in her life.

Renee went home and got absorbed in her daily routine. It was only when she was alone that her thoughts turned to Kunal. She found herself thinking often of him these days. One morning she emerged from her bath, humming her favorite tune from her College days :

Aaja piya tohe pyar dun

Gori baiyaan tope vaar dun....

Her heart was singing once again and she smiled at herself as she brushed her hair; the dimple on her left cheek was back. Gradually she realized that without meaning to, she had fallen in love with a married man. She felt the caressing warmth of Kunal's love; she was never lonely again. She began to eat better and slept more soundly. Although she was married to Rajdeep and shared her life with him, in all the years they had lived together, he had never understood her.

Renee wondered what her *Dadaji* would have thought if she had confided in him. She remembered his advice when she had fallen from the swing in Bareilly, when she had been six years old, "It's not falling that matters. What matters is getting up again." She understood the one thing her *Dadaji* would have told her: it was important to go on living, clutching at whatever straws one gets to hold. Her grandfather would have encouraged her to embrace life, to accept whatever was offered and to make the best of it. He would, perhaps, have told her not to bother too much about what other people might say.

From that day onwards, Renee became conscious of Kunal's physical presence: she could almost smell his mixture of talcum powder and after-shave lotion. She found reassurance in his strong, male voice even when he was talking to another person or when she heard it from a distance in their building. Renee's calm acceptance of his love was like a balm on his own childhood wounds. Kunal needed a woman's caressing softness to heal the pain he had carried in his heart since his school days, even as he went about negotiating his way in the harsh outside world, achieving material success, as well as having a family he loved. His wife Manvi was there, of course, but she could never reach the inner-most depths of his being, where Renee had managed to squeeze in. Kunal was happy, but he had to answer the important question: what was the way forward?

CHAPTER 18

STARS IN HER EYES

Renee confided in her friend Anita about her feelings for Kunal. She had feared her childhood friend would judge her harshly but to her surprise she understood immediately why such a thing had happened in the first place. When Anita had known her in Manduadih, she had been a bold eleven year old, who had not been afraid to venture out into the streets of Varanasi searching for her treasure, with the loyal Sacchu by her side. Renee's family had moved to Calcutta and the friends had lost touch. When they met again, Renee had confessed to them about her innermost insecurities and the trauma of being separated from her mother at the age of three and a half. Her mother had not been there to nurture, or to provide her and Jatin, with a sense of security. As she had grown older, Renee's bold and adventurous nature had made her plunge headlong into troubles of many kinds. Her closest friends, like Sara, had understood what a bundle of contradictions she was: bold but insecure, wanting to try out new things in life, but her courage failing her at the last moment. Kunal had first met her as a young woman; he had begun to like her, but she had got married to Rajdeep and begun a new life. Renee had crossed swords with her in-laws and ended up losing Rajdeep's sympathy in the bargain.

Anita could empathize with Renee in her search for security and happiness. She realized the only way forward for Renee was to stay away from Kunal, and to immerse herself in activities which would keep her busy. She told her to apply for a teacher's job in a primary school. The next day Renee visited a school nearby with her resume. As luck would have it, they had a vacancy in the Primary section and asked her to join immediately. Although Rajdeep was surprised by her sudden decision to start working, he accepted it gracefully, and did not make much of a fuss about it. Renee quickly adjusted her daily routine, so her household chores were taken care of in the mornings before she left for school; she changed the maid's timings. In school, she had been given the responsibility of teaching students of class two, and enjoyed her work from the first day. Her own sons were becoming more independent and fitted in effortlessly with the changes in the household.

Kunal had not seen Renee since the evening he had gifted her the book. Where was she, and why was she avoiding him? He wanted desperately to see her again. He saw her children playing every evening with Nikita and Ayush when he returned from work, but she was never around in the lawns these days. Was it possible that she was trying to avoid him? If so, why? He had not seen her for almost four weeks and he was getting restless. Where was Renee? That evening, returning late from work, he ran up the steps swiftly, just to be able to see the door of her flat. He heard an old Hindi film song playing inside, perhaps on a T.V. show. Kunal felt a moment of panic: was it possible that she had confided in Rajdeep? There was the definite possibility that she had decided to save her marriage. He had to know immediately. In rising panic, he pressed the doorbell. She opened the door, and saw him standing outside: his lips dry, his face ashen, pleading with his eyes, for an answer...*Do you love me?*

She stood in front of him, blocking the door, not asking him to come inside. She looked up at him, standing there, looking so vulnerable, and spoke wordlessly with her eyes, *Why are you afraid? It's you I love. I have told Rajdeep nothing.* She spoke in the universal language of love and he understood immediately. She gestured towards her husband with a slight tilt of her head, as if to say "Look! He's watching T.V. and I was fixing dinner." It was as if she had spoken to him; each understood what the other was trying to say.

Kunal regained his composure, and the color returned to his face. Rajdeep had lowered the T.V. volume and joined Renee. "Oh! It's you Kunal!," he greeted his friend, "Haven't seen you for some time. Come in and join me for a drink."

"Later... Manvi will be waiting for me, I got delayed in office today," he said, turning to go. He ran up the steps, all the way to his flat.

Kunal was trying to grapple with his own feelings: why had he been so upset? He could not understand why he should need a married woman's love to feel complete as a man. Why had he been so scared of losing Renee? He sat back in his office chair and closed his eyes, and he was once again the frightened twelve year old boy, hiding behind the door and hearing of his father's grave illness. He needed the gutsy school girl of Manduadih to hold him and tell him, "Kunal, what is there to be afraid of?" He finally understood why it was said that women were stronger than men and why, with all his achievements, he needed Renee. If the eleven year old school girl, chasing fearlessly after her treasure, had met the sixteen year old Kunal in those days, she would have taught him to have no fear in the world. She would have made him feel the cool Manduadih breeze on his face; the young boy in Kunal held on tightly to her hand, and became stronger by the day; he was no longer angry with the world. His face glowed, and there was a new spring in his steps. Best of all, he had regained his boyish smile.

After returning home from school, Renee went about her household chores as usual. Rajdeep noticed she had started looking happier and her old self confidence was returning. He thought it was the effect of her new job; he knew the importance of keeping busy, and he was relieved to find her in a better mood. He was having a hectic time himself: shuttling between his regular job and visits to Alipore to help his parents sort out their problems. It was becoming increasingly difficult for them to see to the upkeep of their large house and they depended heavily on his support.. Abhishek and Gaurav accompanied him on holidays and enjoyed the pampering of their Dada and Dadi.

Once a year, his elder brother Ashok came with Pallavi and Sonia for a visit. He stayed like a guest, and was polite to everyone but showed no interest in his parent's affairs beyond that. He had never forgiven *Bauji* for humiliating him in front of his younger brother and sister, and the entire household staff. He no longer felt any sense of involvement with the activities of his parent's house. Thankfully, the cousins Abhishek, Gaurav and Sonia were the best of friends; they were unaware of, and also unaffected, by the conflict among the adults. Sonia, being the eldest among them, was full of stories about her father's postings in the various cantonements and the two boys listened wide eyed to her.

They, in turn, made her part of their various exploits in the garden and made her play the role of either a queen or a house help depending on the play of the moment.

The months went by, with occasional meetings in the building or the enjoyable Sunday lunches at the Tollygunge Club. Both Renee and Kunal were careful to keep their feelings to themselves. Their spouses were unaware of any relationship between the two of them; they made it a point never to meet outside alone. They were two married people who had discovered they needed each other: yet their new found love posed more questions than it answered. While they basked in the glow of being in love, Kunal was becoming increasingly aware that he would need to take a call on the way forward; he had a family he cared for deeply and he was well aware of his responsibility towards them. A man did his duty first.

Kunal and Renee became aware of how deeply they were in love one evening, at a dinner party thrown by a common friend of theirs. Rajdeep and Renee arrived early, and their hosts greeted them warmly, and ushered them into the large drawing room of their eighth floor apartment. Renee looked beautiful in a grey and green sari, with pearl eardrops and a matching string around her neck. She chose to sit on a double-seater sofa with two of her friends, while drinks and snacks were being shown around. Kunal and Manvi arrived a little later, and were welcomed by their host. As he was introducing them to the others, Renee rose hurriedly and in the confusion, her sari pallu slipped from her blouse, exposing her cleavage. The creamy skin of her beautiful bosom glowed like silk against her dark blouse and Kunal stood rooted to the spot: he could not take his eyes off Renee. She blushed and struggled to free her sari and covered herself quickly. Kunal collected himself and moved on with his wife to greet other people in the room.

The party was on in full swing; talk was noisy as the finest of drinks flowed and delicious snacks were shown around. Everyone was having a good time. Renee stood near the window of the tall building, peering at the pavement below. She could see cars parked in a row shining in the soft street lights and the neatly trimmed hedges of the small gardens. Beyond, she saw the wide expanse of the Calcutta Maidan, the lights shimmering in the distance. In the street below she noticed a hand rickshaw standing tilted under a lamp post, two men on bicycles riding leisurely engrossed in conversation, and a few cars speeding on the empty roads. Renee felt at peace as she had never felt before in her life; all her anxieties and insecurities had disappeared. Having finished her dinner, she went to the dessert counter and took two hot gulab jamuns and a scoop of vanilla ice cream. She sat on a chair at a distance from where Kunal was sitting, talking animatedly with a group of men, as they finished their last drinks before eating dinner.

Renee wanted to keep sitting there, hearing Kunal talk, hearing him laugh and enjoy himself with his friends, seeing him so happy. Their eyes met and he could see their were stars in her eyes and she was telling him, "I love you." He nodded and gave a soft laugh. I'm in trouble, he thought, I've fallen in love with a married woman. Kunal knew he would have to do the honorable thing. The responsibility fell on him; he knew Renee would look to him for guidance. He hoped he would have the courage to do the right thing for them and their families.

CHAPTER 19

Rahen Na Rahen Hum

A few days later, Renee saw Kunal one evening going out with his family. They were walking towards the car park and her heart skipped a beat, as she watched him: how handsome he looked in a brick colored shirt and beige trousers. She could see the new happiness in Kunal, the spring in his steps. She loved him and wanted him to be happy.

Once again, their life took on a predictable pattern of daily routine, yet they were both aware that they wanted to get closer; Renee wanted to be held in his arms, and lay her head on his shoulders, and forget all her troubles. She hoped some day Kunal would muster up the courage to ask her to meet him alone. She waited for that all important call that never came. Kunal dared not get closer to her; he knew he would not be able to control his feelings once he was alone with her. After a lot of careful thought, Kunal made a decision.

He rang up Renee one afternoon, and asked her to meet him at the lobby of the Taj Bengal Hotel in Alipore, around five the next evening. Renee had been expecting Kunal to approach her, so they could discuss the way forward for the two of them. She rarely lied to Rajdeep, but that evening she told him one of the teacher's in her school had invited her for her birthday celebrations in her home the next evening, and she would be going for it.

Rajdeep muted the T.V. show he had been watching, and asked, "And the boys?"

"They'll be playing downstairs," replied Renee, "I'll see to it that they finish their homework in the afternoon and give them their evening snack early. Just make sure you come home by six o'clock."

"All right," said Rajdeep, "Remember to tell the durwan to keep a watch on them."

"I will," Renee assured him. She knew there was no need for that as Abhishek was responsible enough to listen to her instructions and keep an eye on Gaurav as well.

The next evening Renee dressed with care in a green kurta with beautiful embroidery in the front panel and matched it with a lemon coloured churidar. She applied eyeliner and lipstick and put on a small bindi. She smiled at herself in the mirror and went to fetch the boys from their room where they had been playing a board game.

"Are you going to a party Mummy?" asked Gaurav.

"Yes" she replied, "It is my friend's birthday.. Let's go downstairs where both of you can play with your friends. Be careful, the two of you," she warned them. "No fighting, and Gaurav you listen to what bhaiya says. Dad will be back soon."

"O.K." they replied in chorus.

They took the lift and went out into the lobby of their building, from where Abhishek and Gaurav rushed off to play.

As she stood outside her building gate an empty cab came by, and she sat in it and told the driver to go to Alipore. The roads were just beginning to fill up with the office traffic, and they made it to their destination in thirty minutes.The security guard of the hotel let the taxi drive inside the premises to the imposing porch. She alighted, and counted the change and paid the driver the exact amount. She loved the ambience of the five floor hotel which had creepers growing in flower beds all along the frontage of the rooms; they were falling enticingly down the ledge, with little white blossoms which shone from a distance. The   gateman, dressed in churidar and kurta in crimson, gold and white, opened the glass door with a flourish and ushered her in, with a bow. Suddenly, she was standing in the lobby, bathed in golden light streaming in from the fifth floor atrium. Huge columns supported the roof, and the palm trees and potted greens placed all around gave a feeling of open spaces. Renee had been here before; yet, she was filled with delight each time she came. She looked around the elegant décor, the light coloured upholstered sofas where people were sitting in small groups and talking. She was wondering whether she should go to the reception to inquire about Kunal, when she spotted him walking towards her.

"Hello Renee!" he greeted her with a smile. His heart skipped a beat as she looked up at him trustingly, looking so pretty.

"Hello Kunal!" she said, "I hope you've not been waiting long."

"I came about ten minutes ago. Come," he said, as he

stretched out his arm behind her shoulders and ushered her towards the coffee shop. "Let's have some tea."

The coffee shop was on the right, towards the back of the hotel, from where one could see the large outdoor swimming pool, and the lush green lawns, edged by flower beds and thick bushes. The atmosphere inside the coffee shop was one of comfort, and the round tables covered with printed tablecloths gave a homely feeling. There was a round porcelain vase containing pastel coloured flowers amidst an abundance of green leaves in the centre of each table and quarter plates, tumblers with folded napkins, and cutlery arranged around it. A few of the tables were occupied and they sat on the chairs at a four seater. The steward came for their order: he asked for a cheese puff for himself and a chocolate pastry for her, and a pot of Darjeeling tea for both of them.

As soon as the steward left, she came straight to the point, "What is it Kunal? Why did you want to meet me?"

"I've been thinking, Renee," he said thoughtfully, "About us. About Rajdeep and Manvi and the children. What is the best way forward for all of us? I can never hide anything from you. Not now, after having known you for so many years. I trust you implicitly and I know you do the same."

"Tell me, Kunal," she said earnestly, leaning forward.

"Not here," He replied firmly. "Perhaps we can walk in the lawn outside...."

"No!" she interrupted him quickly, "Let's go to the Agri-Horticultural Garden, near Lakeview Park. I used to go there for walks when we lived there. It's huge and there will be plenty of privacy."

"All right," he said. "Let's have some tea first."

He poured out the tea in the cups and she added the milk and sugar, half tea spoon for him and one for herself. Both were quiet, as they sipped the hot brew. It was the quiet which comes from years of knowing each other and of feeling complete with the other. It only happened when a man and a woman loved each other, never otherwise. Once they had finished their tea, he paid the bill, and they rose to go. She wanted to use the washroom before leaving, and he waited patiently for her in the lobby till she returned. They walked out of the hotel towards the car parking and he opened the passenger door for her to take her seat. He drove towards Alipore Road, weaving his car through the busy evening traffic, but the distance was short, and they were soon near the gardens.

When they reached, he parked opposite the Lakeview Railway Colony, where they had first met. As they walked, they passed Penn Road on the right, which had some majestic private houses and a beautiful housing complex, Sakchi House, of a large steel company. They went inside the huge horticultural garden with manicured lawns, trees, shrubs, rows of neat flower beds and a variety of potted plants. They crossed a quaint little wooden bridge, which had been built over a narrow water body, next to a small pond, on which floated water lilies and a few lotus flowers. There were two wooden benches under a shady tree, overlooking the pond, of which one was occupied by a young couple holding hands and deep in conversation.

They sat down on the empty bench and Kunal turned towards

Renee and put his hands on her shoulders. It was the first time he had touched her. He came straight to the point, "I'm leaving Calcutta, Renee!"

"No!" she cried, shocked.

He put his arm gently around her shoulders. "I've already accepted another job in Bombay. It's a well-known firm and they are providing me housing in an upscale area and have increased my present drawn salary. I've resigned from my job here; we leave in two weeks ."

"Why Kunal? Why this sudden decision?" asked Renee in an anguished voice, tears stinging her eyes. She pleaded, "Stay back...don't go."

He shook his head sadly. "I have to go, Renee. There is too much at stake; the future happiness of two families is involved. Our children deserve the best...I know you want that for your boys."

"I do," she nodded, sobbing, "But I also want to be with you."

He took out his handkerchief and gently wiped her tears. "Our love is like a treasure," he said, "with the help of which you and I can face the future. Remember, Renee, in life, duty always comes first. It is not only love; there is also honour and duty. The lucky ones get to love and stay together. We are not eighteen and twenty, *na*, Renee. I'm a married man and you are a married woman..."

"...I know that," she interrupted him, impatiently. She was silent for a while. A few minutes later, she said in a soft voice, "We can lead our own lives; we can meet sometimes."

He shook his head. "We can't do that...*log baatein karenge.*

Aur hamaare beech baat badhegi na, Renee."

"To kya baat nahi badhni chaahiye?"

"No," he replied, calmness and strength in his voice.

She pushed him away. "I hate you, Kunal!" she wept.

He lifted her face by the chin.

"Look at me, Renee. You love me enough to want me to do the right thing. I know what a strong woman you are. You can face anything the world throws at you. You will never be alone. My love will always protect you, wherever you are."

She nodded quietly. She knew Kunal well; if he had made up his mind, he was not going to change his decision. She trusted him implicitly, even more than she trusted herself. She could make a wrong decision, swayed by emotions, not him. That was why she had admired him in the first place, and fallen in love with him. He was so sure of himself: if he had decided the best thing for them to do was to go their own ways, she would have to trust him.

"Hold me close, Kunal," she said, "Enough to last me a lifetime." He put his arms around her and held her tightly, as if he would never let her go.

He buried his face in her hair and whispered, "I'll always love you, darling."

He could feel her clinging to him, pressing her face against his chest. "Don't go!" she entreated.

"I have to," he replied, his voice tender, "I know you love me enough, to let me go." She relaxed in Kunal's arms, feeling the old strength seeping back into her flesh and bones. It was almost as if the strength she was seeking was coming to her from Kunal's touch, slowly percolating into her innermost depths. After a while she loosened her hold and let him go.

"You're right Kunal," she said. "Neither of us can ever be happy if we don't do the honorable thing; in that respect we are alike. Go to Bombay. Trust me, I'll not try to contact you. My love will always protect you."

He rose from the bench and held out his hand to her. "Let's go, Renee. It's getting late." She stood up and after settling her clothes, took out a brush from her purse and combed her hair. She gave him a smile, her one dimple showing. How beautiful my Renee looks, he thought, and I have to let her go.

As they walked to the gate she said, "I'll take a cab...we should go home separately."

"No!" he said with determination. "I'm not letting you go alone, so late in the evening. Come with me in my car."

She was afraid. "What if someone sees us?"

"So what?" he asked. They had reached his car and both took their seats. "There's nothing to be afraid of Renee, when we've both decided we're going to do our duty."

She looked at him lovingly, even as he focused on driving home through the conglemoration of cars, two wheelers and buses.

Chapter 20

Renee's Triumph

Abhishek opened the door for her, as soon as she rang the bell. "Where were you Mummy? We're hungry and we have school tomorrow."

"I'll fix your dinner in a bit. Just give me time to change," she replied, as she hurried to her room. She could hear Rajdeep and Gaurav in the kitchen, trying to make a snack.

She hurriedly put away her new churidar kurta set, and wore the old salwar suit she had been wearing in the day time. She took care to remove her bindi, wipe her lipstick and eyeliner, and splash water on her face, so that Rajdeep would not notice anything. When she reurned to the dining room, Rajdeep had switched on the T.V. and the three of them were eating the French toast he had made. She heated the vegetable curry she had cooked that morning and kept in the fridge, and took out the bowl of kneaded dough to make hot parathas.

"Dinner's ready!" she announced ten minutes later, as she brought in the hot curry. Abhishek helped her bring out the dinner plates, bowls and spoons. "Wash your hands both of you, and let's eat."

The boys eagerly described their day in school and Rajdeep told them about his latest project at work. Later, in bed, while Rajdeep fell asleep immediately, she lay awake thinking about Kunal and his shift to Bombay with his family. To her surprise, she did not feel alone any longer. She felt Kunal's presence, as if he was holding her close to him and whispering, "I'll never leave you." She turned to her side and slept peacefully.

News spread in their building that the Chopras were shifting to Bombay. Rajdeep expressed surprise at Kunal's sudden decision. He had assumed he liked his present job in the steel company; perhaps he had received a better offer he found too good to refuse.

"We must take Kunal and Manvi out for a meal before they leave," he told Renee as she sat doing corrections of the pile of exercise books, she had brought from school that afternoon.

"Alright," she said absentmindedly.

"I forgot to tell you...next Sunday we are having lunch at Alipore. I promised Ma I would bring all of you along."

Renee continued to accompany her husband to his parent's house, but her relationship with her mother-in-law was one of indifference, at best. *Bauji* had grown older and frailer and was always kind to her and Renee reciprocated by showing him the utmost respect. Other than that, she sat like a guest and rarely commented or participated in their conversation. Abhishek and Gaurav enjoyed the pampering and having the run of the house till they were called for lunch. Mrs. Varma had been watching her daughter-in-law's growing confidence with great suspicion. She noticed how her body language had changed: she no longer walked with slow steps and lowered eyes. Her head was held high, she had a new glow to her face and she looked altogether more self assured. It must be that teacher's job of hers, Mrs. Varma thought to herself. She's not even qualified for the job, she must be getting a pittance for a salary. I'm sure she'll not go very far with it. Can she ever compare with our property and wealth? She will always be financially dependent on my son. She can put on as many airs as she wishes, I'll see to it that my son puts her in her place.

Everyone collected in the dining room for a sumptuous lunch, for which all of Rajdeep's favourite dishes had been made. Renee tried her best to be pleasant, and went to the kitchen to fetch hot puris for *Bauji*, for which he blessed her with a smile. The boys ate the delicious food with relish, and Renee was glad to see them enjoying themselves. After early tea, Renee was relieved when it was time to go back to their own flat.

The next week packing began in tbe Chopra household. Kunal went to office to wind up work and hand over charge, and he made a number of trips to the children's schools to get their transfer certificates. Nikita and Ayush stayed at home and enjoyed all the chaos, even as Manvi tried to keep her house clean amidst the gunny, paper rolls, bubble wrap and cartons spreads all over the place. She had been taken aback at Kunal's sudden decision to resign and had tried to argue him out of it. After all, they were well settled in Calcutta, it was a nice friendly city, the children went to the best schools: he would hear none of this. His mind was made up; they were moving to Bombay. He assured her she would like the city and make friends there too.

Renee wondered what her parents would have thought, if they knew she had found support outside her marriage, to fight her battles in life. Once a year she went with her sons to visit them in Lucknow, but she no longer discussed her personal affairs with them. *Mamoni* noticed Renee was looking healthier and gradually regaining her old confidence; she too assumed it was the result of her job as a teacher. The very fact that she was stepping out of her home and going to work, and earning money as well, must be acting like a tonic, she thought. She never said anything about it, but was pleased to see her daughter happy again. Renee's brothers Jatin and Sonu had found jobs and were venturing out on their own and she rarely met them on her brief visits.

The Chopra's packing was completed by Tuesday evening, and loading began the next morning. It being a week day, Rajdeep left for work after eating his breakfast, having dropped Abhishek and Gaurav to school by car earlier in the morning. Renee had taken a day off from school, to catch up on pending work at home. When she was a young girl, she had frequently been in the midst of the chaos and excitement of the move to another town: the goodbyes and the eager anticipation of new beginnings. This morning she stood forlornly at her window watching Kunal supervising the loading of his furniture and other cartons on to the waiting truck. She felt bereft as she watched him, dressed in white shirt and blue jeans, giving instructions to the men as they lifted the heavy packets, and handed them to the two men standing at the edge of the vehicle.

They never did get to take them out for a meal, although Rajdeep had tried to contact Kunal a few times. Kunal and Manvi were too busy attending office farewells and doing last minute shopping before leaving Calcutta. Renee understood

Kunal was doing his best to avoid another meeting, and she was immensely grateful for that. When she had said goodbye to him many years ago in Lakeview Park she had not imagined they would meet again and in circumstances which would bring them so close. It was time to say goodbye again: it was what he had asked her to do. For her, Kunal would be her hero, even from a distance of hundreds of miles. He would be there to guide her through the most difficult times in her life. She felt his hands on her shoulders, and heard him whisper, "You are a brave girl and that is why I love you." It was Renee's triumph that she could let Kunal go to do his duty towards his family, while she turned away with a smile to do her own.

Chapter 21

The Real Treasure

After Kunal and his family left Calcutta, Renee felt very alone. She prayed to God to teach her acceptance and to make her strong again. She diverted herself by keeping busy at school and in household activities. Even if Rajdeep saw her looking wan and quiet, he kept his apprehensions to himself. Every evening she crossed the busy main road in front of her house and went for a long walk on the pavement, among the many pedestrians rushing to get home. She walked briskly for about a kilometre, then turned back and returned home. The thronging crowds and their animated talk among themselves, and the fact that she had to constantly manoeuvre her way among them, seemed to calm her, and make her forget her pain temporarily. She had not realized she would miss Kunal so much; her grief was tangible and real.

About a week later, she had a vivid dream in the early morning just before waking up. Renee was back in her school in Howrah and had completed her Senior Cambridge examinations. The results had been declared and *Mamoni* was looking for someone to go and fetch her mark sheet. Kunal was with them and he offered to go. "I'll get it," he told her mother. He returned empty handed saying, "The

school has changed, the staff has changed." No one seemed to bother about the news; they are elated, as Kunal and Renee have recently been engaged. He has given her a small diamond solitaire ring and she is very happy. Renee woke up with a start and looked at her ring finger: she was wearing a solitaire she had bought from her teacher's salary. She immediately understood the meaning of the dream. She would have to face the world herself, with Kunal by her side. She never felt alone again and her sense of sorrow left her. The spring in her steps returned and she could smile again and share the little joys of her children. That was the reason why Kunal had come into her life: to teach her how to live. He would have wanted her to move forward with courage in her heart and a smile on her lips.

Renee realized that the real treasure was life itself. It came as a package deal; you got some, you did not get some. There was no point chasing after what you were not meant to have. So much better to find contentment in the given, and the present. The important thing was simply to keep going, even when the sun did not shine brightly in your little world, knowing full well some day the clouds will lift and let the sun's rays in, and the rainbow will appear in its full glory.

Renee knew what she wanted to do next. Once the household was settled and her sons were in school, she took a taxi to the Bank where *Dadaji's* gift, the diamond encrusted pen, had been kept in a locker. She was going to take it out and write her story. She wanted to share her journey with others, about living with courage, and being the person you were meant to be. One had to find a reason to keep going, even when one's life was full of hardship. She wanted to tell her story in which love and hope had triumphed over every other obstacle and proved to be a beautiful journey.

Made in the USA
Monee, IL
22 October 2020

45849576R00115